SURROUNDED ON THREE SIDES

A Novel by

JOHN KEASLER

Foreword by Les Standiford and Diane Stevenson

SURROUNDED

ON THREE SIDES

University Press of Florida

Gainesville Tallahassee Tampa Boca Raton Pensacola Orlando Miami Jacksonville

3 1969 01097 6594

04 03 02 01 00 99   6 5 4 3 2 1

LIBRARY OF CONGRESS CATALOGING-IN-PUBLICATION DATA
Keasler, John.
Surrounded on three sides: a novel / by John Keasler;
foreword by Les Standiford and Diane L. Stevenson.
p.cm – (A Florida Sand Dollar book)
ISBN 0-8130-1710-6 (pbk.: acid-free paper)
I. Title. II. Series.
PS3561.E247S87   1999
813'.54—dc21   99-20678

The University Press of Florida is the scholarly publishing agency for the
State University System of Florida, comprising Florida A & M University, Florida
Atlantic University, Florida International University, Florida State University,
University of Central Florida, University of Florida, University of North Florida,
University of South Florida, and University of West Florida.

University Press of Florida
15 Northwest 15th Street
Gainesville, FL 32611
http://www.upf.com

FOREWORD

John Keasler was both a journalist and a novelist, known for funny and sometimes biting satire in both genres. During his thirty-year career at the old *Miami News*, which ended when the paper folded in 1988, he wrote nearly 7,000 humor columns—one per day, five days a week—as well as the satirical "By George" and "Ryan the Advice Dog." But his editor, Howard Kleinberg, also sent Keasler to cover the major historical events of the time—Kennedy's assassination, Neil Armstrong's trip to the moon—because Keasler was, in Kleinberg's words, both brilliant and a fine writer.

When John Keasler died in Plant City, Florida, in 1996 at the age of seventy-four, he was remembered by the *Miami Herald* as having left behind "a legacy of love for his home state." That love, combined with the kind of concern for Florida's future expressed by his contemporary, John D. MacDonald, is what makes *Surrounded on Three Sides* a privilege to reprint in the Florida Sand Dollar Series.

In this 1958 novel, Paul Higgins, a New York public relations man, grows sick of his cold and artificial world and moves to fictional "Flat City" in rural Florida, somewhere west of Okeechobee, somewhere east of the west coast. There he sets out to fulfill his dream of becoming a writer, only to find his newfound paradise threatened by developers. Using his PR skills, Higgins devises ingenious and hilarious ways to discourage people from moving to Flat City, in an attempt to stem the tide of "progress" and defend Florida against those who would commercialize and plunder it.

Surrounded on Three Sides, with its satiric tone and now-familiar theme, occupies a unique place in Florida fiction. Its zany, on-the-mark characterizations and its insistence that no developer's scheme is too preposterous to attract zealous backers presage the later, darker work of such writers as Carl Hiaasen and James W. Hall. Often violent, humorous, and fundamentally moral, this strain of Florida literature chronicles the struggle of a singularly beautiful landscape and environment to maintain and preserve itself—not against such natural destructive forces as the cycles of hurricane and drought, but against the unnatural erosion caused by human envy and greed.

Les Standiford and Diane Stevenson, Consulting Editors

With love to Margery; of La Belle

"Now, then. What do we call a body of land surrounded on three sides by—*are you paying attention to me?*

"Yes ma'am. What do we call a what?"

Overheard in a geography class, Mitchell Elementary School, Tampa, Florida, 1931

MEMO TO READER

FLAT CITY, FLORIDA, AND ITS general locale are fictional. My own home town, Plant City, Florida, is way farther north, in the heart of the strawberry country. It is growing by Leaps and Bounds. My wife's home town is down in South Florida all right, and in tomato country, but it isn't Flat City either.

Flat City and its residents simply do not exist. Not any more.

John Keasler
Ferguson, Missouri

CHAPTER ONE

Palmettos fidgeted lazily in the soft breeze of southern inland Florida, and nowhere was there hurry. In this cattle and farming area, flatlands unpopulated to the point of eeriness, lay Flat County, west of the big lake Okeechobee; east of the Gulf and its tourist-teeming highways.

Flat City, the county seat, had a population of 1,495 persons, no Chamber of Commerce and no particular interest in growing to 1,500. Newcomers were made welcome to a degree dependent on the individual newcomer, but newcomers were not sought. However, with the month of April in 1958 came a strange rumor and Police Chief J. S. Williams thought he was the first to hear it.

He walked briskly into Flat City Pharmacy, wearing the smugly portentous look of a man with a shiny new nugget of gossip. He poured himself a cup of coffee from the Silex, stirred deliberately and noisily until Druggist Bake glanced up from his

Wall Street Journal (Flat City was only geographically rural; spiritually, it was cosmopolitan) and said irritably, "Don't wear out the dime-store cups. They're heirlooms."

Casually, still stirring, Chief Williams said, "Guess you've heard the old Space place is being sold."

"No!" said Jim Conklin, who worked at the feed store, and who was standing at the magazine rack thumbing through the photography magazines in his never-ending search for naked women. "Who to? Smithsonian Institute?"

"Nope" said Druggist Bake.

He smiled thinly at a point over Chief Williams' head.

Then he said, deflating Williams' role as town crier, "Somebody's going to live there. Yankee woman was down looking at it yesterday. I hear the deal's practically through."

Chief Williams frowned, and vengefully put three more spoonfuls of sugar in his coffee, stirring furiously.

Then, seeking his lost prestige, Williams said, "Old Willingham down at the paper said the fellow buying it is a New Yorker, in public relations."

"In what?" said Mrs. Perkins.

"He must be out of his mind," said Jim Conklin.

"Oh, I don't know," the druggist said. "It's got mighty fine timber. It's well built. Old Ronald Space bought nothing but the best. And me, for one, I never thought Ronald was near as crazy as they said."

"Ha!" snorted Williams. "He was strictly for the squirrels. Remember when they fined him for shooting fish and he said he shot them because he couldn't stand to take the hook out? And how he tried to file charges against the State Game and Fresh Water Fish Commission for encouraging cruelty to animals? By not letting people shoot fish?"

"That must of been the year Alfred and I were in Europe," Mrs. Perkins said, sipping her cherry phosphate.

"Hell," said Jim Conklin. "A fish ain't no animal."

"Tell you one thing," said Druggist Bake slowly, pulling at

his mustache, which he wore as a prop in his capacity as town sage. "Whoever bought that place is an individualist. A downright one."

"I was trying to think how much old Space got fined that time," Chief Williams said, trying to think. "Can't remember. Quite a bit, though. I remember he paid it all off in Indian head pennies."

"Yep," said Mrs. Perkins, "that must of been the year Alfred took me to Europe. He said he always wanted to ride on an ocean. 'Alfred,' I said, 'Alfred, let's go while we can. None of us are getting any younger.' And we went! He hated every minute of it."

Jake Baldwin, who owned the feed store, waddled in, his face round and enigmatic. Jim Conklin took one last look at Nude in Tree and sidled out. Jake hooked his thumbs in his belt and said importantly, "Well, folks, hang on to your hats. I got news."

The news moved fast through Flat City, that April. *The old Space place is sold . . . .*

The old Space place was four miles out of Flat City, on Devil's Lake where the Withlahatchee River fed in. Some folks had wondered what ever would happen to the Space place, but the wonder had been diminishing with the years as it became evident that nothing, apparently, was going to happen to it.

When Ronald Space had been alive, the rumor had been that Ronald—who was known as Harrington Space's crazy brother —had a gold bathtub in his home. A young real estate editor on one of Harrington Space's newspapers once gained fame— of a nature even more temporary than most fame, inasmuch as he was promptly fired when he sobered up—by calling up Harrington Space's crazy brother long after midnight to ask a question. The newspaperman had an inquiring mind. He was a seeker after knowledge.

"Mr. Space?" he said, when Ronald stumbled sleepily to the phone. "Tell me. What is the best way to get a ring out of a gold bathtub? I got to worrying about it, and couldn't sleep."

"I know you, John Riley, you son of a bitch," said Harrington Space's crazy brother, Ronald, who was a far cry from being crazy. "I'm going to tell my brother on you."

He did, and Harrington Space fired John Riley, not out of any sympathy for his brother but because Harrington Space had a firm rule about staffers charging long distance calls to the office.

John Riley, who had been working on Florida newspapers for years without ever getting caught up on his car payments, went into the real estate business and in a relatively short time made so much money he turned Republican and received ovations at luncheons by saying N.R.A. stood for Nasty Reds Association.

Ronald Space, who had started with one dragline and made a quarter of a million dollars in drainage work in the Everglades area, died a couple of years later on a drizzly August day in 1942, the result of absent-mindedly chopping a tall Australian pine down on himself.

Ronald had been a prolific writer. It was, in fact, his hobby and pastime there in the big house where he lived alone in south central Florida. However, his writing had been largely limited to what he termed Outdoor Sonnets, plus a few miscellaneous essays denouncing such organizations as the Rosicrucians and the American Medical Association and he had failed to get around to composing and writing a will.

His estate, more or less by default, went to his brother Harrington. The estate consisted, as far as anybody ever found out, of the huge house he had built in the most deserted part of Florida he had been able to find; a gallon jar nearly filled with Indian head pennies, and a list in unbreakable code headed: "Savings Accounts, East of Mississippi."

The huge old house rared above the grove of scrub oaks which were raffish in hanging and tattered Spanish moss. There were many trees of many kinds in this flat wild country

Ronald Space had chosen. The big house looked out over the big black lake and the Withlahatchee River curled through one corner of the land. It was a disheveled house. After a couple of years things began to fall off it. Harrington Space forgot he owned it. He had many properties in progressive areas. And he was occupied with his newspapers.

His newspapers, both dailies and weeklies, spotted Florida. Harrington Space considered himself the William Randolph Hearst of the Sunshine State, or at the very least the Joseph Pulitzer. He knew little and cared less about the section of Florida where his brother had built his crazy house.

Harrington had few subscribers and no advertisers at all in that section of Florida, simply because there weren't many people in that section.

Main highways also etched across the interior but none came through that part of Florida. Ronald Space had built his castle in solitude and the highways turned away the invaders, like a moat.

He was far from the coast where the surf called the Yankees, far removed from the Tamiami Trail with its whizzing tourists, far south of the ridge country with its bustling citrus gamblers, far north and inland from the neons of Miami.

Even during the first boom the outside world had hardly touched Flat County, Florida. When the 1950's came, after Ronald Space was gone, even the second and much larger boom didn't touch it either. The only tourists to get into Flat City were bemused individuals who had taken a wrong turn in Fort Myers or somewhere.

These individuals, irritably, would ask a Flat City native what became of the broad highway. The native would point silently back whence the outlander came. The tourists would roar away.

They were in a hurry to get to Florida and brooked no delay; humping over the wheel, zooming through Flat County.

Greenly and serenely Flat County lay, quietly and anciently

calm. Hump-backed and indolent Brahman cattle munched at tall, untrodden St. Augustine grass. Moist mango trees gave shade and ripe guavas fell, plump, where no ear heard.

The sun beamed peacefully on the lakes and the land, and the moss swayed.

Far away, this way and that, the black-etched highways were busy. Flat County picked deep-red tomatoes and munched them with a little salt, lying back under a lime tree and eying the soft sky for showers.

Its people were a breed no Florida-seeker ever knew without first being fully accepted. It was a self-contained little town. Its citizens had a serenity. Their faces were tan, their hands were hard and their humor was tongue-in-cheek. Except for the young men, few Flat Citians ever went to Miami. The older folk seldom even went to Fort Myers.

Flat City had taken the many and varied breeds to arrive at its site and in an astonishingly short time blended its own personality type, recognizable to even the most obtuse, an individualistic personality—unique. Adventurers had built this town, as adventurers built San Francisco, although neither would have welcomed the comparison.

Flat City was a cracker town. There is no easy definition for a Florida Cracker. The literal-minded say he is simply a Florida-born native. This has nothing whatsoever to do with it. A man can be a Yankee and a Cracker in the same lifetime, although it is true only a limited number of men are equipped to do this. Most of these, however, end up as Crackers. The rest wonder all their lives what is wrong.

Arthur Bake, for instance, who ran Flat City Pharmacy, had lived until he was forty-two years old in Pittsburgh although now those years seemed to him like a murky dream. And now that he was seventy he wasn't sure but what they had been. His son, born in Florida, right in Flat City, lived in Orlando where he was a highly successful embalmer but he would never in his life be a Cracker. His daughter, born back in Pittsburgh, lived now on Park Avenue with a Yankee broker husband but she would never be anything but a Cracker.

The term is not easy to define. You are or you aren't. A Cracker is inclined to gamble, and knows when it's going to rain.

Like San Francisco, Flat City had a large first or second generation population. Families had come from places with exotic names like Racine and Providence. Some of the tribal elders had snapshots of snow. The kids equated snow with brownies—they believed in it, but it wasn't real.

Around Flat County for a period of years after Ronald Space's death one of the favorite pastimes of the children was playing in and around the old Space place. It was a fine place to play although, sadly enough, years of effort had failed to furnish the house with a believable haunt.

One reason may have been that it is difficult to envision the average ghost having much of a sense of humor and Ronald Space, in his own way and despite himself, had possessed a sense of humor. Warped, perhaps, but definitely there. Or, at least, a sense of the ridiculous. Naturally, his house imitated him.

For one thing, the house had no front door.

It had a screened porch, a big one. But it had no front door. The front wall went straight across. There was a deep psychological reason for this. Ronald Space only liked back doors and side doors. He didn't like front doors.

This, in years past, had been the cause of deep frustration to the occasional country peddler or salesman who all unawares dropped in. It is a rending experience for a journeyman front door knocker to find no front door. Ronald never explained the lack, or addition, whichever it was. He never explained anything. And, having picked his homesite well, he was not called upon to explain anything.

Flat City had its normal share of idle curiosity but it was leavened with a facet of its own personality. Flat City did not give a happy damn, not really.

Flat Citians, the breed, demanded little conformity. Adventurers—even inadvertent adventurers—never do. They merely accepted the house, as they accepted the sun and the summer rain, with an unthought-of awareness. The house was just there, as is. The legend about the gold bathtub was dead; the first assault wave of children after the house became vacant disproved that story. The bathtub had only a peculiar, comfortable backrest, done in waterproof gilt.

The years clawed at the house ineffectively, for it had sturdy rafters and thick walls and its cypress had served a long apprenticeship standing in swamps, and cypress knows how to ignore time, better than most things.

It was a big house, of many rooms. One could get lost in it. Halls stopped for no particular reason.

It seemed to swell in the second story, giving it somewhat the look of a stockade; actually the second floor *was* larger, due to a tight-lipped feud Ronald Space had carried on with the architect and builders.

Space, dissatisfied with the architect's plan, had insisted on laying out the plans himself for the second floor. The architect's pride was wounded, but his bank account was low. He had compromised with his art to the extent of muttering, all right, let the bastard try it.

(The architect was already shaken by Space's insistence on, among other unorthodox innovations, no front door and by the demand for a trap door in the parlor floor to sweep dirt into.)

Consequently the first- and second-floor plans of the dwelling were done independently of each other. Space and the architect had ceased to speak to one another. When the puzzled contractor attempted to point out that the two floors didn't seem to fit, both Space and the architect, independently, told him not to get bogged down in details and to get on with the job.

The builder was enchanted by this problem and did the best he could. The result was the stockade effect with overtones of Moorish dome. The house looked as if it had some strange organic swelling in its upper reaches or as if the attic were packed too full. The builder, an Irishman, of some creative pride himself, ended up speaking neither to the architect nor to Space until finally the only common communicative ground was a Flat City native named Funnelthroat Freely who worked that summer as a carpenter. Funnelthroat was an ant rather than a grasshopper, working faithfully each summer so he could stay inebriated the rest of the year; one of the few village drunks entirely self-supporting in this age of creeping socialism. The builder followed plans to the letter and as a result the completed house had no stairway from the first floor to the second.

Ronald Space did not deign to notice the oversight. He had a staircase built outside, on the opposite side of the house from the chimney, feeling it lent a nice balance; also lending impetus to the idea that he had wanted an outside staircase, rather than that he had forgotten any staircase at all.

The architect later came down with severe hypertension in the midst of designing a Christian Science edifice in Jacksonville.

After Ronald's death, and after the house acquired that atmosphere of public property which surrounds all long-empty buildings, children used the outside staircase as a shot tower, melting solder in a tin can with a blowtorch and dropping the molten metal in droplets to a tub of water below. The slingshot pellets were fine for small game and insulators.

So, it was bad news that came in April to the local small fry—that somebody was going to live in the Space place. To some of the older fry, who played their own games down near the lake and the river on the lawn at night, it was bad news also.

("But we'll always think of it as *our* place, won't we, Stu?" inquired a Miss Annie Mae Timmson on a moonlight April night on the grassy lawn by the century plant near the front porch. "Yeah," said Stu. "We better go now, though. Your old man thinks you're at the Baptist Young People's Union.")

The curiosity around Flat City had mounted, for even in this latest of Florida's booms few Yankees moved to Flat City.

"I always hear about public relations men," said Baldwin to Druggist Bake. "Exactly what does a public relations man do?"

Everybody thought it over, but nobody knew.

They discussed it, with growing interest, there in Flat City Pharmacy, and they offered various theories, and the argument mounted in intensity.

"Oh, a public relations man is *not* an advertising man," said Bake, in reply to Chief Williams. "And he's not just a press agent. He's—well, I—it's . . . oh, hell."

"Well, it all sounds mighty suspicious to me," sniffed Mrs. Perkins. "My husband's cousin never could explain exactly what he was doing, either. Two men from the government came and took him away one day."

"Ha!" said Williams. "Here comes Willingham. He'll tell you, Bake—you're such a know-it-all!"

Editor Theodore Willingham of the Flat City Ledger walked in, nodded. He was a tiny, white-haired man with startlingly blue eyes under white eyebrows thick as caterpillars.

"You worked on big-city papers," said Williams. "Tell Bake here—what does a public relations man do?"

Editor Willingham thought it over at length. He shifted his tobacco from one jaw to the other. He concentrated on the question. He finally said, "You know, I never *did* find out."

That was in April; Flat City lay quietly and undisturbed, under the peaceful sun.

CHAPTER TWO

. . . In the dark ages, wandering minstrels
were made welcome at great castles because
of the influence on public opinion they were
able to exert on behalf of their patrons . . .
Public Relations
Encyclopædia Britannica

NEARLY THREE MONTHS BEFORE
that April, on a New York sidewalk, and through the freezing
drizzle of a February afternoon, Paul Higgins stalked along;
wondering where the time had gone, for today he was forty-
five.

Click! went a stop light.

DON'T
WALK

"Run," replied Paul Higgins, straight man to the stop light.
He walked across the street against the light, thinking of the

clicks of the city; the click of his heels, click of the machines, all the clicks, clickety, clickety: I myself am a machine, he thought. Fed certain coins, motivation, I will produce certain things, function. I will go *click*.

A fragrant girl wearing a fuzzy red coat passed him swiftly clicking on high heels. Who are you? he wondered. He considered a cigarette, but he had smoked too many cigarettes getting through the lunch conversation.

He was a big man, 195 pounds, six feet and he seldom laughed out loud. His hair was thick and at forty-five, exactly, some gray was in the black but it looked black; needed cutting. When he walked he walked erect, moving his head a little from side to side, to see. He never carried a briefcase, but he was in public relations.

A siren wailed in the city. Going to fix a click, he thought. He walked along, his head turning a little, looking at the city. He went to his office, Creation, Ltd., where he was a creative vice president.

He was seated at his desk, worrying about being forty-five, when in came Arthur Rodes, tall, thin, easy-moving, grinning like a thieving fox. Arthur was a creative vice president also, but Arthur thought it amusing.

Arthur looked like a riverboat gambler with a perpetual ace in the hole. He smoked long thin cigars. All he needed was a string tie. When he had been a newspaperman he had been a careless dresser; now he was neat but not dapper. In his college class picture he had been the only graduate with his arms folded. He knew about contrast.

"WearPruf!" Art barked, poking his cigar at Paul like a rapier. Paul looked at him glumly, half listening. Art had landed the WearPruf account, and was re-enacting the crime; building it into a two-acter.

"So old man Grinson asked me this," Art said, dramatically. "The old shrivel-soul says, 'What can your firm do for me?' "

"That's the one that gives me trouble," Paul said.

Art, pacing, a phony look of dedication on his face, abruptly poked the cigar and said, "I told him, 'Mr. Grinson, public opinion is both fluid and at the same time a malleable solid. We at Creation mould that marriage of the tangible and that which must be sensed!' Pretty good, huh? What the hell does it mean?"

Forty-five, Paul thought. Forty-five, fifty. Fifty-five? Sixty? Sixty? Sixty-five, seventy—here I come, ready or not.

"Well, congratulate me, Paul," Art said. "Even Otto congratulated me on this one."

"I'm sorry, Art. I'm a little low, I guess." Paul, his shoes off under the desk, scratched one sock-clad foot with the other, ran his hand half-irritably through his hair, fiddled absently with his peanut butter glass filled with yellow pencils.

"Just a little mood, kid. You got the old temperament. You'll snap back," Art said.

"I am forty-five today," Paul said. "It's worse than sixty. Thirty was the worst."

"Prime of life, forty-five. Peak years. Let's get fried."

"Not now."

Art went cheerfully back into his act, and spoke at length on opinion moulding.

Paul said to himself out loud, "Once I was on a paper in Georgia and there was an editorial writer, wore sleeve garters, who always referred to himself as a moulder of opinion. Only man I ever knew who spelled Jesus with a little 'g.'"

"Speaking of Jesus," said Rodes, "Grinson was thinking it would be nice if WearPruf could get sort of an Easter message to the public, come April."

"An *Easter* message? About brake lining?"

"I like the way you get right to the heart of things."

Paul said, "Why I'm sure one of the resident ad geniuses could work that out in, as they say, jig time. James A. Wedley could do it in real jig time. How about a good slogan, like 'Some Church Goers Don't Know When to Stop.' Have a picture

of this convertible running over Norman Vincent Peale. Power
of positive brake lining. Look, Art, I have a little hint."

"Go away?"

"I like the way you get right to the heart of things."

Art Rodes exited, snapbrim and cane. Paul grinned, thinking: The crazy, nice, thieving bastard. He walks the surface of
this earth as if it were the Texas deck of a sidewheeler.

Then Paul stared at his desktop, bare and very neat. Not alive
and sloppy any more. He had a bankbook and he had been
making an entry when Art came in; more money than he had
ever dreamed ten years ago, even five, that he would ever own.
The bankbook lay on top of a promotion plan young James
A. Wedley had brought in for approval. "You Can Put Your
Trust in Sparkilite."

Trampled by trivia, my epitaph, Paul Higgins thought;
nibbled to death by ducks. "Nibbled to death by ducks!" he
said loudly. Sock-footed he walked to his window and looked
down on New York 17, N.Y. Why, he asked himself, don't I
ever have that urge to jump, like the psychiatrists do?

At forty-five on his February bleak birthday he wanted to go
somewhere, do something. But I am locked in the castle belfry,
he thought, picking a stringless lute.

The phone rang. The phone rang all the time. It was James
A. Wedley who wanted to skeet-shoot and zero in. James A.
actually talked that way, and if Paul hadn't read John Crosby's
columns and several dozen satirical novels on public relations
and advertising he would have thought James A. lost and
sinking. Paul told James A. he would like to help him get the
flat trajectory but he was all tied up. Then Paul got the liquor
out of the cabinet, jiggled his pencils in the tall glass, and
wondered what to do. He called his wife.

"Maybe you better come in this afternoon," he said. "I've got
the whimmies. Maybe we better celebrate."

"Maybe we better," she said.

Mrs. Higgins, Betty, hung up absently. She had never seen

him exactly like this. Many ways, but not like this. She wondered how it would feel to be married to a contented man. Doubtless, she decided, the source of never-ending discontent.

"Lou," Betty said to her eighteen-year-old daughter, who was arranging magazines on the glass-topped coffee table. "I don't suppose your schedule permits, by any freak of fortune, staying home with Junior while I go out with your father?"

"You *know* Jamison is coming over at five and we're going to Little Theater," her daughter said tightly. Her daughter was interested in theatrics and often talked in italics. Sometimes her daughter said *simply divine*. Betty was always surprised.

"O.K.," Betty said. "I'll see if I can get the sitter."

"A *sitter* for that slob?" Lou said, casting her eyes toward heaven and pointing to her brother without looking. "A *keeper*, yes. A sitter, no."

"That's no way to talk to your brother," Betty said, ritualistically. "Junior, will you please turn that TV down?"

"You'll have to speak up," said Junior, ten, very witty. "I can't hear you for the TV."

Betty Higgins said to herself: "I'll get Mrs. Wheeling." Mrs. Wheeling was the sole support of her brother in Utah who had been dying slowly for thirty-two years. "Junior," Betty said, walking toward the kitchen, "did you take a bath?"

"Why? Is one missing?"

"Oh, *God!*" wailed Lou.

"Lou!" said Betty.

Her daughter ignored her and leaned over, in her tight shorts, creating an effect Betty deemed near obscene; although it wasn't the shorts' fault, it was Lou's. She made even loose garments seem clinging. Bending over, now, she was seeking the proper effect, determining if Dramatic Arts and the Writer should be on top, or the Nation and the Reporter. She settled by leaving a copy of The New Yorker, open, over all of them.

The phone rang. Betty answered. It was Alma Vannington. Alma wanted her to be on a book drive committee. She accepted. Listening to Alma and trying to concentrate on what she was saying was like trying to remember to be careful when standing in the bathtub. Alma finally hung up.

Betty walked to the refrigerator, and opened a can of ale. The PTA meetings, she thought. The Garden Clubs. The "Community Seminar on Juvenile Delinquency," which ended with Bill Vannington, who was in corporate relations, doing his imitations and falling into the pond with the ducks.

She shook her head, sitting there on the kitchen stool, looking at the shiny-shiny of it all. Once the accumulation of money for a second-hand washer had been glory, and its breakdown disaster. Now she felt like a picture in Good Housekeeping.

She was a slender woman, not yet forty-one, self-contained, who dealt with the whips and bitcheries of life quite well. Her eyes were clear and green and her face was quick to laughter; there was femaleness in her walk, and men watched her often.

She had been married to Paul Higgins for twenty-one years. In that time, she thought, a man is many men. Basically the same man, of course, but he revolves, slowly, showing new and different facets. He is on a slowly revolving base, powered by flowing time.

Why, she thought suddenly, surprised at her own surprise, he has given up writing even an occasional short story. Because he doesn't have the time. Because he has become preoccupied with security. And put childish things away. But he is hungrier than ever, she thought, tossing the empty ale can deftly into the trash can: And where can he explode to from security?

"This is *my* town," she remembered a younger Paul Higgins saying. They stood on a bar on a rooftop and looked down at a new city where he had a job paying $10 more per week than the job in the last city; they had a bank account of $85, of which $50 was due for rent, and were going to have a baby, hooray! The town had been San Francisco and they had conquered it, although only the two of them knew it; a better job had taken him to Cleveland, then they stormed Chicago, too, and a couple of other fortresses. Time powered the base, though; the need for security came. And now we have oodles of security, Betty thought, and we have come to think in quotes: "Place where your roots are," and "It's to the best advantage of the children."

We have just gobs of security, she thought, walking toward the bedroom to change for the city. Then why is my husband hungrier than ever? Because he has merely changed uniforms again? Sometimes when Paul was drunk he attempted to explain about the uniform, and how he knew the precise instant he had put on a new one: First the bush-jacket, no-hat attire of the college intellectual; then the upturned hatbrim brashness of the city room. He always changed as soon as he found he had one on, he said. But the uniform will get you if you don't watch out—the sweatshirt phase when he was free-lancing. Then the Army. The only time he had been out of uniform, he had said, was when he was in the Army—then, belaboring the point, he lost it.

Now he had been ten years in public relations. But he didn't know how to get this one off, Betty thought—this is the one with glue instead of buttons. And I am afraid of the current battlefield, she thought—for it is eating my husband up in little bites. Every day he has to get on the train with those other men and go prove again *every day* something he shouldn't be proving at all.

"But we've got everything," she thought, in quotes, undressing, taking the green dress from a hanger. "This is what we've worked for."

I've got to quit that, she thought. So, I'm worried about my husband. So? He'll work it out. What a nice tribute to him, she thought; that I'm worried about him, but not too much.

He is not *either* a penguin! she thought—and damn my sister for that comparison, anyhow.

Her older sister, Louise Antel, who lived in Florida, had

come to visit them two years ago and stayed two weeks, which, Louise had said wryly, was all she could stand of Slathesdale, N.Y. The first morning Louise had ridden in to the commuters' station with Betty to take Paul, Louise had solemnly surveyed all the solemn men on the platform, each with his paper and his likeness of brow and each all buttoned up.

"My God, they're *penguins,*" Louise Antel had said in hushed, awed tones. Then she had thrown her head back and laughed like hell.

Well, he is not! Betty thought angrily, undressing. Abstractly, she turned and was startled by the near naked woman in the mirror, with her brows pulled together and her lower lip stuck out. Hm, Betty said, stepping out of her pants; not at all bad for a more or less junior-matron penguiness. She did a fine lewd grind climaxed by an excellent bump; turned sideways to survey her full-length nude profile.

"Muh-thurrrr!" her eighteen-year-old(!) daughter squalled from downstairs. "Jamison's mother wants to know if you'll be at the next delinquency seminar Wednesday night?"

It was after five o'clock, the retreat hour, in the offices of Creation, Ltd., and Art and Paul both had their shoes off, high above the cursing and raving and drizzly·streets.

Rodes drank bourbon and wondered what female would be most appropriate to. help him celebrate Paul's birthday. He decided on a lady fur buyer, a charming woman who had been introduced to him by his ex-wife whose taste Art had always admired. Occasionally, when his alimony check was late being mailed, Art sent his ex-wife a single perfect rose.

Paul drank rye and waited for Betty and ran his hands angrily through his hair and lit a cigarette on the filter end.

Art, his thumbs hooked in his vest, the thin cigar dead between his teeth, said, "The trap complex, Paul. That's all you have. So say we all of us. It is in the scheme of things. I will think of an appropriate quotation.".

Paul said, "I don't want the cheese any more, I just want out of the trap. Mickey Mouse."

As Art, basically the actor, droned on sardonically, happily, Paul looked at him objectively, thinking: Con man incarnate; seal smooth, ancient as speech.

He and Art liked each other greatly. Neither man had any kind of friend but close, and few of those. Each valued the other highly. Art was the salesman, tops in his profession; Paul was not overly articulate, but came through with ideas. Together they were a fine team and Otto Anvel, head of Creation, paid them each exactly $2,500 a year more than either could have gotten individually at any other top firm. Plus bonuses. They were Mr. Anvel's inventory and he knew where he could sell them. Art thought this was shrewd to the point of wickedness on the part of Otto Anvel, and was vastly amused. Paul thought it was merely good business, but was appalled by the idea. The two creative vice presidents, whose thinking dovetailed neatly, were dependent on one another—the slickness and the spade.

Rodes, ex-newspaperman, had come to love public relations and advertising—Creation did both—and to revel in them. Higgins, ex-newspaperman, had come to dislike them immensely.

What happened in a few short years? Paul asked himself. Once I was going somewhere. Now? Well, he thought, I must be here already. He wrote material for clients and the typewriter at home sat quietly.

At least, he thought, I am "Providing Very Nicely for My Family." He never talked about writing any more, because he couldn't stand the smart boys' smiles.

"Take writing," Rodes said, telepathic as always. "You don't have the right approach. Those stories you used to sell. They were O.K., mind you. But why bother? Be practical. Write a best seller."

"Thank you for pointing the way."

"Scoff if you will. But wait until my book is published. Sex, don't you know—but not the same old stuff. This one will appeal to both the high-minded and the lascivious."

"How? Pull down the shades during fornication?"

"Primitive, unworthy of you. Now, think of all the four-letter words you know."

"Four, scow, onyx, beer, five, moot, toot, root—"

"No, no, no. *Obscene*. Mencken said there were thirteen. I think. Never can get that many myself. But I will run a survey. Now here's what I'm going to do."

Carried away, pacing again, ad libbing, Art delivered his formula, "Two kinds of readers," he explained. "First, you have the droolers, the vicarious—thrill lads and lassies who get right in that sack with every verb and adjective. Secondly, the reader who likes a good story but doesn't really care, simply for the sake of rung-in sex, who is laying who."

"Whom."

"Whom. O.K. So what do we do? We put all the obscenity on the flyleaf! A list of the four-letter words; one master-key description of a bout in the pad, a few miscellaneous phrases to cover deviates, perhaps a handy reference list of the letters of the alphabet. Dirty-minded can have a do-it-yourself field day! Clean-minded can simply tear out the page! In there?"

Paul said, "Leave blank spaces here and there in the book. Lead-in sentence says, 'So Herman and Hilda lay down under the pecan tree to rest.' Reader can write anything he wants to."

"In there, man, you're in there!" Art shouted. "Think of the sense of power!"

Paul said, "On the cover you could have a detachable sticker saying 'Flyleaf banned in Boston.'"

"Lord, we're rich. Rich, rich, rich," Art shouted.

"Contest," Paul said. "'Sexiest homemade passage in 25 words or less wins a pony.'"

"We're artists, artists!" Art bellowed. "Rich artists, that's the best kind! I quit! Where's Otto?"

Paul said, "Book title: 'Your Flyleaf Is Open.'"

Art moaned estatically, "MGM will fall—"

"What are you two so noisy about?" Betty Higgins asked, opening the frosted-glass door.

Paul had been laughing for the first time all day. He looked at his wife and she looked so suddenly young and hopeful, in her green dress and wide hat and leather coat, that it hurt his heart.

"What's so funny?" Betty asked, smiling.

"Quotations," Art said, looking at Paul looking at Betty. "And if I laugh at any mortal thing 'tis that I may not weep. Father Time. Let's go celebrate before he goes under again."

Art obtained his lady fur buyer and they celebrated. The two couples parted after midnight. Betty and Paul went to a bar on top of a tall building. He liked places high up. He looked down at the dark and fabulous city and wondered what he had thought to find. What had the eagerness been about? What had he done with himself? Other than put his trust in Sparkilite. All my thoughts, he said to himself, are trite, and my emotions are quite confused. But—I certainly do want out.

She was watching him. She said, "We've got plenty of money in the bank, Paul. We could do what we wanted. Go where we want. To Florida, maybe, as Louise keeps insisting."

"And do what? Farm? Buy a weekly? What?"

"You're a good writer and you were going to do that."

"Everybody was going to do that."

"You're different."

"Sure. Real different." He drank his brandy and looked at the neat line the coat of his uniform made in contrast to the white cuff of his sleeve. He shrugged his epaulets and looked at the city. It was 1:15 and he was forty-five.

"Let's go home," he said, suddenly cheerful. "The mood's gone. It was just a mood. I better get some sleep. Tough day tomorrow."

Why, hell, he thought, "I don't know how lucky I am."

CHAPTER THREE

Cliff Tipton that February, 1958, slept motionless as an oyster and as untroubled. Awakened abruptly, he picked up a sentence where he had dropped it, in the middle.

". . . a damn sight better than vodka!" he said, loudly and dogmatically, attempting unsuccessfully to remember what the first part of the sentence had been.

He opened his eyes and the sun bit in. He clawed at the sun.

"Daytime again, I suppose," he snarled, and as his eyes began to focus he shrieked, "DOUBLE DAMN! GET AWAY FROM ME!"

The fat woman in the polka-dot playsuit jumped back like a dainty hippo affrighted.

Cliff Tipton, unshaven, skin color of copper, wearing purple trunks, fell back in the canvas beach chair and put his hands over his eyes. "No way to live," he whimpered. "This is no way to live."

"I do hate to intrude," the massive woman said. Her fat bare

32

toes toed into the beach sand for flight.

"What's a damn sight better than vodka?" Tipton asked himself. "Where did everybody go? What time is it? Is this Friday?"

"One o'clock Friday," the woman squeaked. "This Friday. I do hope I didn't interrupt your nap, Mr. Tipton, but the girls back in Detroit—we *all* bought your book—just won't believe I really saw and talked to you unless I get your autograph and I *do* hope you don't mind."

Tipton took the proferred pencil and paper and scribbled, "Thanks for those passionate nights behind the General Motors assembly plant, Cliff Tipton," and, folding the paper in the middle, handed it back.

He struggled erect, took his bearings and teetered away toward his house back in a palm grove. He was a big, square-framed, large-stomached man, in his fifties, grizzled and sinewy-legged. When he walked he rolled like a sailor.

Adoringly, the fat lady from Detroit clutched her autograph to her polka-dot halter and watched the famous author depart, scratching himself under the armpit and scratching at the sandy stubble on his bulldog jaw.

Cliff Tipton shut his door behind him and kicked his way through his littered living room toward the kitchen, stepping over a bored cat. He went straight to the refrigerator, big as a bank vault, and peered in. On the top shelf of the refrigerator were eight cans of beer, six cans of onion soup, a long-billed beach cap and a side of venison. Hurriedly he opened a can of soup at the wall opener and tried to drink it.

He spluttered, looked at the label, put the soup back in the icebox, opened a beer and called to his wife out on the breeze-way, "Trudy, what the hell is onion soup doing in the icebox?"

"I don't know," she called back. "What is that baseball cap doing in there?"

"It's not a baseball cap, it's a beach cap," he said. "What time did everybody leave last night?"

"I don't know. I went to bed early. Are you hungry?"

She was a handsome, leathery woman who accepted her husband and her life, liking and loving both with gentle and tolerant forbearance, and entirely unperturbed by either. She prepared bacon and eggs and he ate large quantities. They had three cups of coffee each, together on the breezeway, and at four o'clock he sat down at his typewriter to work. He worked three hours at a stretch, at least, although no particular three hours, every day but Tuesday, getting up only to go to the bathroom. He did not like to work Tuesdays.

Their home was long, low, spare and efficient, utilizing much screen and the shade of many pines. It was on the tip of Guava Springs Key in the Gulf of Mexico a few miles south of the City of Guava Springs on the west coast of Florida south of St. Petersburg and north of Bradenton. Once the key had been deserted and now it was crowded. This was a source of anger and heartache to Cliff Tipton.

During that afternoon and early evening the following individuals came to the back door, which faced the Key Road and which people thought was the front door: (1) a pair of stenographers on vacation and seeking autographs; (2) a young writer who was cynical; (3) a man who had invented a two-wheel locomotive and needed backing to buy some single track and (4) the program chairman of a civic club across the bay in Guava Springs, who wanted Cliff to be corresponding secretary and head of the publicity committee.

During the same period the following individuals came to the front door, which faced the beach: (1) an intellectual; (2) a writer friend of Tipton's who woke up in the garage and wanted a drink of water and (3) two more pudgy ladies from Detroit.

Also during that period a total of four automobiles stopped on the hard road and the occupants looked at the house where the famous author lived.

Although none of these strangers actually managed to interrupt Tipton, he was aware, and annoyingly so, of their presence. Trudy turned them all away, gracefully, simply by saying Mr. Tipton was not in. But nevertheless Tipton knew they were there. They were part of the terrible truth.

His oasis, his beautiful sandy key, had become a "resort."

His key was invaded and lost.

Bulldozers ate like fat piranhas into the sand making places for more "developments" and subdivisions. The west coast belonged to pale foreigners in polka-dot halters and baggy trunks. They had taken the land and put up rental properties called Surf'n'Something and built the houses called "No Tengo Rancho" and the cottages called "Happy Holler" and the motels called God knows what and other pale people came and listened to the Red Sox on portable radios on the wide beaches; Guava Springs Key had tourists and all the wildness was gone.

Cliff Tipton sat in the sand, backed against the gulf and, futilely, snarled.

When he had come to Guava Springs Key there had been one rickety wooden bridge, back in the 30's, and few sober motorists ever tried to cross it. Now there were two concrete bridges and another under construction.

Cliff came to Florida a newlywed. It was his third marriage. Two women had previously divorced him as impossible to live with. He had encouraged them in this. His third, and permanent, wife, Trudy, had—instead of divorcing him—sensibly suggested his irritability and unpredictable way might rise out of the fact he was miserable in his position as assistant credit manager for a Sears Roebuck store in Chicago.

He moved, with her, from Chicago to Tampa and found her suggestion had been valid. He spent days on end sitting and watching Tampa Bay and wondering why he had lived in Chicago in the first place. Then their money ran low. In 1932, and also in 1933, he found no job he wanted.

He sold graveyard lots for a while, worked at a shoe store and with this experience landed a fairly good job as assistant buyer for an imported-olive concern. He met a man who operated a deviled-crab stand at night and was a writer in the daytime. The man sold a story to Black Mask Detective for $40. He had made it up out of his own head.

Tipton, impressed, tried his hand at pulp writing and did quite well. He was prolific. Many of his plots hinged on ingenious ways husbands had of murdering wives. During this period he typed the husband's called-for comeuppance on the end of the stories with the greatest of reluctance. Most of the locales were Chicago. One story was titled Mail Order Corpse.

His stories sold well and in the midst of the depression he became solvent. He decided to write a book, because he wanted a boat, and did so.

Slowly it became evident to him that he was not a credit man, basically, but a writer. One night he and Trudy and a newspaper couple from Bradenton drove across a rickety wooden bidge to a place called Guava Springs Key where the newspaperman advised was situated the only trustworthy bootlegger in the area who would be available at 4 a.m. on a Sunday.

Everybody, including the bootlegger and a lady who was visiting him, went swimming that early morning. The moon was big and the sunrise awesome and the beach was the broadest and whitest Tipton had ever seen.

Fiddler crabs scuttled in red-brown freedom. Pelicans rocked on little waves at dawn. The air smelled green. He consciously enjoyed breathing instead of merely having to do it. The beach sands drew a broad curving line through eternity, each way you looked.

Nobody lived there. Tipton built a house and wrote seventeen books in it, some of which sold quite well.

He didn't mind the years because he aged slow and well, like cypress. But he hated the "progress" which, when it came, came like fast idiot ants, hungry and unreasoning.

He didn't believe they would ever crawl out as far as he was. He was a victim of overconfidence, like a too-shrewd delta farmer who eyes the rising river and spits knowingly and says it will never get higher than right there and who is later drowned with his crops.

Cliff Tipton could not grasp the inconceivable—that the west coast of Florida would be overrun, and he with it, and that—indeed—he did not own it but had merely gotten there first.

Ignored for many years as a writer, he was now very famous. His last book had been a runaway best seller and sold to book clubs and to the movies for a fabulous price. Hollywood and television and the paperbacks pawed competitively for his earlier books. When he went places people pointed at him and when he stayed home they came and stared at him.

Guava Springs Key became the place where Cliff Tipton lived. Artists and writers came.

It was decided that Tipton had been an important writer all along. People asked him what he had meant by the mesage in the C.O.D. Murders, circa 1939, and compared it to the enigma in "The Lady and The Tiger." He said he hadn't been able himself to figure out who done it. They laughed and said he was a deep one, all right.

People came and interviewed him bodily after his latest book walked off with the important and terribly significant prizes. He told Time, Inc., he had gotten his writing experience by doing the lingerie copy for the Montgomery Ward catalogue, an untruth. He told a lady feature writer for the Miami Courier that he had quit writing until he recuperated from a recurrent case of satyriasis, which information certainly gave her copy-editor a start.

"Well, he *said* it was like gall bladder," she said.

He had a certain fun with his fame but always he resented the invasion of his home. But the Northerners had discovered Florida's west coast at last, learned that water was on the other side from Miami, also, and that it came right up to the shore.

Beach cottages to the right of him, now, and to the left within easy screaming distance a glass-brick cocktail lounge.

Where once were only mangrove swamps and the happy singing frogs at night now were going up eighty-three more new three-bedroom low-down-payments, carport and a "Florida room."

The old palm trees spread their arms and shuddered in the noisy breeze.

Down at Blackjack Cove where once lived only a claustrophobic bootlegger and a man whose pride in life was that he had embezzled $2,250 from the WPA, was a yacht harbor. (Carrot-Top III, Sea Nymph, Out to Launch.)

Now it was 1958 and Tipton, the famous author, quit working and scratched his month-old beard. He hadn't gotten much done. Nothing, in fact, except writing a letter to the Surfside Bakery threatening to stop eating bread if the delivery truck man didn't quit blowing that damn whistle every morning. He had gotten nothing done, but he had stuck it out the minimum three hours. It was habit started in the terribly insecure days and now a fetish. When literary people asked him the secret of writing success he said it was to write two or three hours every day, except maybe Tuesday. They just laughed.

He ambled out into his living room and said hello to the cat.

"Shave," his wife commanded.

"Why?" he said, alarmed. He never had to shave unless they were going somewhere. "Where do we have to go?"

"To Harrington Space's party and we'll be late so hurry," she said. "And shut up. You accepted, not me. I told you you would be sorry."

"Oh God," he said. "Well. All right."

He shaved with a straight razor, recklessly. He stood before the mirror, sinewed legs apart, belly touching the washstand. In shorts he looked like a circus roustabout except for no tattoo. Dressed, he looked like a carnival owner with quiet tastes.

"Harrington Space," he said reflectively. "Now there's a suethead for you."

He sat on the bathtub rim, tying his shoes. "Hey!" he said. "I can tell people I'm working on my 'short novel.' "

No reply.

"You know," he shouted, "Hemingway goes around saying he's working on his long novel. I can say I'm—"

"Get dressed," his wife said. "That's the first time I ever heard you rehearsing gay social lion repartee."

"First time I ever had a half-million dollars," he said, and laughed loudly. "You know. Like in the talking dog joke? Fellow bet he could send his talking dog down to the drugstore and it would bring back a can of Prince Albert? Gave the dog a dollar? Dog stayed gone and stayed gone? Fellow went looking for it and found it in the alley with a girl dog? Fellow said Fido I'm surprised at you, this is the first time you ever did anything like this. Dog looked back over his shoulder and said, Hell, boss. First time I ever had any money."

He heard his wife backing the car out.

"No sense of humor," he said, opening the refrigerator for a beer to take with him. What the hell is this cap doing in here? he thought. Well, he decided, I might as well wear it. It's already cold.

Trudy drove and he sat beside her going down the hard road toward the concrete bridge. Neon flickered on both sides.

He said, quietly, "Trudy, this breaks my heart."

"Mine, too," she said, also remembering frogs. "Should we move?"

"A man shouldn't have to move again," he said. "Anyhow, move where? Where's left?"

"I don't know, Cliff. I swear I don't."

In the far North, tangled netlike in a clammy sheet, Paul Higgins that night tossed and muttered.

CHAPTER FOUR

HARRINGTON SPACE APPROVED OF culture. He was delighted that Florida was getting lots of it.

He was a firm advocate of the arts. Music and painting and writing, etc.

From time to time, when he happened to think of it, he would send out mimeographed memos to the editors of his newspapers demanding, "What about art?"

He called this "jacking the team up."

But tonight the pressures of business, as he put it, were behind him. He sat in an iron chair on his broad patio and said to the executive editor of Space Publications, "Rick, Florida is rapidly becoming the veritable nesting grounds of the arts."

"You're right precisely, Chief," said the executive editor. "I never thought of it that way. Had you, Jerry?"

"Nesting grounds are for the birds," muttered Jerry Space, Harrington's son and heir, a thin young man whose shoes were of suède. Jerry's head turned slowly and his small eyes became less bored as he watched the passing of an adequately busted young thing who twitched by toward the grove where the party lights were strung. She was a busy walker. Her derrière would have been the envy of a filly in horsefly season.

"Ain't no flies on her," said Jerry contemplatively.

"Nesting grounds was but a figure of speech, Jerry," his father explained. "I do wish you weren't so literal-minded. You must get it from your mother. A newspaperman should cultivate his imagination. You need imagination, Jerry."

"I got it," said Jerry, his head still turning. "Believe me, I got it."

"Someday, Jerry," Harrington Space said, solemnly, "you'll have to take over."

After leaving an Eastern college—after leaving several Eastern colleges, in fact—Jerry Space had come home and been put, over his howling protest, to learning the newspaper business "from the ground up." His father had turned him over to a back shop foreman and the latest lesson Jerry had learned was not to put his hand in an automatic job press when it was in operation.

He was now learning the circulation end of the business.

"Yessir," his father said. "You'll have to take the reins."

"How?" inquired Jerry, holding up his bandaged fingers. "No hands?"

"Experience," his father said, "is the best teacher."

"Gee, you're a wealth of epigrams tonight, Pop," Jerry said. "However, I must away to the veritable nesting grounds— maybe pick up a little experience. A little teacher is the best experience, eh Ricky?"

My God, thought the executive editor.

Jerry slouched off after the tight dress.

Harrington Space pursed his lips, thinking deep thoughts. "Intelligent lad," he said, "but somewhat disoriented as yet. Doesn't have his feet on the ground."

"He's just young and high-spirited," said Rick, thinking:

That was the trouble with Jack the Ripper, too.

"Think we can make a newspaperman of him, Rick?"

"Sure, Chief! Certainly." *He could cover his own paternity suits if he could just get the alphabet straight.*

"Think I'll send him to the Defender-Scimitar down on the coast. Let Williamson start teaching him the news end of the business."

"Excellent idea!" *Plant close to the ocean, good—he might drown.*

Harrington sipped a glass of port. He looked like a successful friar. His face was red and round and assured. He walked, and even sat, with assurance. He was a rich man and getting richer and had been in that happy state for quite a while. He had looked upon the world and found it good.

He owned his chain of newspapers, the circulation and ad rates of which were growing with the increasing growth of Florida. He believed in progress.

He owned radio and television interests, also.

He considered himself a self-made man and, indeed, his holdings were far larger than they had been when he had inherited them. He often said he took great pride in his profession, newspapering. Actually, he had never done any reporting himself, being more the financial rudder.

"A firm, stern hand on the tiller is the important thing in any business," he said all the time, or practically all the time.

His occasional signed editorials attracted wide attention, but his main talent lay in hiring good executives who operated their departments efficiently.

He hired good editors who could hire adequately competent and non-Guild reporters at reasonable wages. Although it secretly distressed him that the news end of the business did not bring in revenue directly, Harrington was aware that news was fairly important in a newspaper. He often pointed this out.

"After all, what is a newspaper without news?" he would

ask. "However, all of us here on the team realize the prime function of a newspaper is to exist and that requires a lot of economy know-how. Nevertheless, the importance of news in a newspaper cannot be overlooked."

Another thing he often said was that he guessed he must have printer's ink in his veins.

His advertising manager made twice the salary of his executive editor.

"What time is it?" he asked his executive editor.

"Nine-thirty."

"Tipton should be here. I know he's coming. My secretary called his wife."

"You know how those writers are."

Space became a man of vision. He leaned back in his chair and folded his hands over his white-coated paunch. "Do you realize, Rick," he said, "what is happening to Florida?"

"No, what?" Rick snuggled up in his chair to hear.

"This is no fake boom!" Harrington said evenly, spacing his words. "This is *solid!* The eyes of the world are on Florida. More tourists! More permanent dwellers who have come to live in the sunshine of the Sunshine State. More cattle! More shipping! More industry!"

"More advertisers!"

"More advertisers! More and more everything. And this time it is a solid expansion. Rick, you are witnessing the greatest mass expansion this country has ever seen. You, with your very eyes as you sit there, are seeing the greatest growth of any area anywhere in the world of today!"

Space took a sip of his wine, looked over the rim of his glass like a federal judge instructing a jury and, waving one hand in a lordly gesture, made his point.

"Rick," he said slowly. "I predicted it all . . ."

The executive editor narrowly kept from clapping his hands.

The executive editor, bow tie and Dacron, looked admiringly

at his chieftain, seer and savior of the Sunshine State.

"Clear eyes and a firm rudder," said Space. "That's all we need."

"Yessiree-bob."

Out under the palms and lights the party was becoming gayer. Laughter had risen to the four-martini level. The string quartet had ceased its dirges and moved into tentative merriment.

Mrs. Space, a heavy-prowed dowager and motherly, moved through the crowd to make sure everybody's glass of alcohol was brimming, as if she were passing out oatmeal cookies. A girlish shriek rose loud and clear and startled in the vicinity of Jerry Space. The quarter moon lay on its back in the soft sky, resting indolently and looking like a section of Valencia orange.

Trudy Tipton turned into the winding drive through the pine trees and moved toward the parking area where a uniformed attendant waggled his arms. Cliff Tipton was eating an avocado and washing it down with a bottle of peppermint schnapps he had found in the glove compartment.

"I can't understand your accepting the invitation," Trudy said, parking skillfully. "And take off that silly hat. Do you want people to think you're eccentric?"

"The son of a bitch appealed to my vanity," Cliff said, taking off the cap and putting it in the glove compartment with the avocado rind and the schnapps bottle. "That's all I can figure. I didn't answer his letter but when I ran into him in Sarasota he buttered me up so I practically licked his hand. Anyhow, I don't know how to turn down invitations. I never think the time will really come."

"Well, it always does. What is this he wants you to write?"

"He never said, exactly. That's why he wanted me at the party. To hash it over, he kept saying. That's what he said, to hash it over. Sounded real significant, like rewriting the Constitution.

My efforts would not go unrewarded, he said. And those were just his words, that my efforts would not—"

"Quit saying what he said," Trudy said impatiently. "I get enough Space clichés in the Guava Springs paper. And, friend, look—you don't have to take hack jobs now. If you will try to recall, you are a wealthy man."

"Well, you get the habit and it's hard to break," Tipton said. "Anyhow, I'm curious. Let's go see. Jesus! They've all got on *coats!*"

"Well, tuck your shirttail in."

They walked across the lighted lawn. Nymphs of stone stood in a fountain.

"If you think that fountain's funny you should have seen who woke me up today," Cliff said.

"Stop babbling. Here comes stupid."

"Well, well, well," boomed Harrington Space, moving rapidly toward them with Rick trotting at his heels. "Well, well, well, well, *well!*"

Tipton shook the plump hand, looking in mild, objective wonder at the sleek and coated bundle of chubby assurance who was Harrington Space.

Editor Rick said, "I read your book."

"Which one?"

"Uh—"

Mrs. Space waddled up and jiggled to a standstill, extended her hand and puffed, "How delightful to meet the Tiptons at last! Why, what a charming little dress, Mrs. Tipton. May I call you Trudy? Call me Grace. Mr. Tipton—may I call you Cliff? Do call me Grace—I read your book. You're a positive genius. I couldn't put it down, could I, Harrington? Just the other day, I—"

"Perhaps they're thirsty, Grace," Harrington Space said.

"Why heavens *yes!*" She banked to the left and shifted to second, high, overdrive. "Right over *here!*"

The Tiptons were steered across the short-cropped grass. Rick trotted along, knowing he wasn't going to like this Tipton one whit. Man looked like a sarcastic bear. And wearing a sport shirt to a supper party.

At the outdoor bar Cliff accepted a martini. One cylinder of his mind chugged on the necessary conversational noises as he looked around in wonderment.

His mind habitually churned out a constant production of temporary answers to things but each new answer brought new questions, much like the rules on how to figure your income tax. Cliff's basic trait was interested puzzlement.

Formal education had puzzled him. His first two wives had puzzled him. Chicago and starfish on the beach puzzled him. Sears, Roebuck puzzled him. He was possessed, owned by, a question-mark-shaped sense of the ridiculous and his laugh often sounded too loud. Often, during the laughter, he would be off in the corner trying to figure what was so funny.

He had written eighteen books and wondered why the last one should bring in all that money as opposed to the other seventeen which hadn't. His own favorite book had been his ninth. It was about a preacher who wanted a green suit. His latest book had been about life as he imagined it might be in a typical small American town.

"Its heartaches and laughter, its happiness and 'tears," one reviewer wrote, "form a massive, moving work which literally brings a community alive, mirroring the lives of individuals against the majestic tapestry of life.

"Refreshing, and long overdue, is the author's refusal to deal in sex for sex's sake. Such episodes as are included are handled with taste and delicacy, an integral part of the whole. We hope this is the beginning of a trend."

Another reviewer wrote: "Mr. Tipton in making a slight and transparent gesture in the thick-slice-of-lowlife direction uses a town populated almost solely, apparently, by adult delinquents as a vehicle for writing about plain and fancy fornication. When will this trend die the death—from pure boredom—it deserves?"

The name of his novel was: That's What Makes Horse Races.

Tipton stood under the palms, vaguely listening to people and considering martinis and our culture. He thought—If a person asks for a very dry martini he is marked immediately as a rather cultured individual, a knowing sophisticate. If he should ask, however, for a martini with as much gin as possible he would be marked a potential lush and never considered for the board of directors. Very peculiar.

"Oh Mr. Tipton!" a woman shrilled suddenly in his ear, causing him to start and slop his martini on his pants front.

"No," he said to himself.

"I adored your book," she shrilled. "Tell me, are you working on another novel at present?"

"Yes," he said, thinking of the bakery man.

"Tell me one thing, do."

"All right."

"How long is it going to be?"

"How what?"

"Your next book. How *long* is it going to be?"

He thought this over briefly.

Then his face wrinkled and his frightening laughter ripped out, great bellows. The woman looked at him in pure terror. All the guests who had been waiting to meet the famous author, waiting until later lest they seem to be unsophisticated celebrity chasers, whipped around and stared at him. ("What was that?" a girl asked, sitting upright in the back seat of a parked car. "Who cares?" muttered Jerry Space. "Pay attention.")

"How *long* is it going to be?" Tipton choked to his wife, through the laughter. "She wants to know how *long* it will be."

And he pointed to where the woman had been, but she was gone.

The laughter soon stopped, leaving a hole in the air. Trudy Tipton went calmly on with her conversation with Mrs. Space and other women. Harrington Space looked blankly at, first, Tipton, who was accepting a scotch and water, and then at Rick, who shrugged.

"Nice night," Tipton said to the two men. "Fairly cool. What kind of grass is this?"

"Why," said Space. "I really don't know. Are you interested in, ah—grass? Gardening? That sort of thing?"

"I guess not," said Tipton. He ate his ice cubes up and the uniformed bartender brought him a bourbon and water.

Tipton asked Space, "What's this writing you wanted me to do?"

"I want to talk to you about that."

"Fine. Let's go over here."

Cliff walked a short distance across the lawn and sat down on the grass with his back against a palm tree. Space and Rick looked at one another. Rick spread his handkerchief and sat down. After a moment Space sat down also, cross-legged.

He maintained a great dignity as the cool wetness of the dew-damp lawn chilled his flanneled bottom. From over where the party was everybody looked sidelong at the three seated men. Tipton, under the orange slice of moon, looked solemnly at Space and barked one cough of laughter; stopped it short, and lit a cigarette.

Harrington Space, cold rump and all, launched directly into his proposal, with the assurance born of long authority.

"I will start at the beginning," he said, "and keep it short. I need a message for Progress Tower."

"What does that mean?"

"What does what mean?"

"That sentence you just said. What does it mean?"

Space rubbed his sleek jowl and showed no irritation. "Ill-phrased, perhaps," he said. "I'll explain. Would you consider composing an inspirational message, aimed both at the present and at posterity, to be chiseled into the edifice of Progress Tower?"

"What is Progress Tower?"

"My God, man!" said Rick in horror. "Don't you read the newspapers?"

"Yes. But I can't ever remember what they said."

"I'll explain to Mr. Tipton, Rick," Space said patiently. "Now Mr. Tipton—may I call you Cliff? Please call me Harrington— Now, Cliff, my enterprises needed a new headquarters building. Many months ago we surveyed the best potential location. Miami was suggested and discarded, as were Orlando and Tampa. It was decided this tower should rise right here in Guava Springs, heart of progress. I decided it."

Rick adjusted his bow tie coyly and said, "All of the chief's advisors, including myself, tried to insist the building be named Space Tower. Harrington, however, is an awful hard man to sway, once he makes up his mind."

"Ye call me Chief," Cliff said to himself.

"What?"

"Nothing. Go on."

The chief recrossed his chubby legs. "No, no, Rick, my boy, not Space Tower. This tall and lofty spire—which should be completed by late summer, barring troubles from that socialistic union—should bear the name of no one individual, it was decided. It should, instead, signify, as will the building itself, the triumph of man's ingenuity and imagination. That's what the name should signify. Specifically, it should be symbolic of the growth—the dynamic growth—of the new Florida."

Space paused, then asked quietly and dramatically, "What, then, to name this erection?"

"How about Surf'n'Sun Tower?"

"Ha ha," Space stated. "Seriously, Mr. Tipton, some message is needed, something of literary worth."

Rick said, "Progress Tower will have a weather ball on top."

"Something of literary worth," repeated Space. "We thought, of course, of going to the classics."

"I practically memorized Bartlett's Quotations," Rick said.

"Very prolific he was, too," Tipton said, eating his ice cubes.

"We decided to rule out the classics for this reason," said Space. "Rick, get Mr. Tipton another rye and get a glass of port for me. And a towel or something to put on this grass. The classics are fine, I have nothing against the classics. Still and all, this thought occurred to me—why not call upon one of our very own literary men of today? Would that not lend added significance?"

"Sure. Why not?"

Space went on, "Florida is becoming a veritable nesting ground of the arts. Think of the fine novelists, short story writers, painters, illustrators, advertising men and so on who live within a bare one-hundred-mile radius of this spot we are standing on. Sitting on."

"I used to know a fellow over in Tampa," said Tipton, "who made real good figures in the sand under the Lafayette Street bridge. People would pitch coins down. Eliminated the middleman. I wish I knew why I got hooked up with an agent."

"Yes," said Space. "Well, I asked myself—who? Who is a writer of prominent standing who lives in the Sunshine State? You, of course, came immediately to mind. It was shortly after my Guava Springs paper had the inspiring interview with you after you took the prize. Incidentally, let me say here and now how much I admired your pluck in learning to write on the back of a coal shovel by firelight. Anyhow, you in all probability are the best publicized author in the United States today."

"What did you have in mind?"

"Well, Cliff—call me Harrington—as you doubtless know, many newspapers have inscriptions on their walls. Great papers like the Chicago Tribune and the Los Angeles whatever it is. These messages—I call them messages—deal, however, for the most part with the newspaper business. Pulitzer, particularly, seemed very preoccupied with it. Now what I want is—"

"Here's your drink, sir," said Rick. "And yours."

"What the hell *is* a weather ball, anyway?"

"The message I envision on Progress Tower should eschew the newspaper business as such."

"That's what I always say. Eschew the newspaper business."

"This building," said Space, "its name and its message should typify the advancement of this great state, should be inspirational, should point the way. So to speak. A rudder to, a tiller of, progress. It should have a theme, a dynamic theme."

"How about progress as a theme?" Cliff suggested.

"Great!" said Space enthusiastically. "Fine. Excellent. You have grasped the point by the horns. I told you he would come through, didn't I, Rick?"

"You sure did, Chief."

"Nothing will make me happier than to know you are busy creating—composing something for this project," said Space. "I do hope you can create it before dedication time, probably in August."

"O.K.," said Tipton.

"Believe me, Cliff, I know you will come up with something good. Something real symbolic, maybe like that writer over in Sarasota, what's his name, did for that Empire State Building outfit."

"Did it have a weather ball on top?"

"One more thing, Cliff—you realize that your efforts will not go unrewarded."

"Forget it. Trudy said I don't need any more money."

"A grand gesture! Oh, a fine gesture. Right in keeping, isn't it Rick? One of Florida's own great artists donating his precious talent to, so to speak, symbolize the dynamic Sunshine State of today. Tell me, Cliff, isn't this the most amazing situation in the history of the old forty-eight? Expansion, progress, amazing. What do you think of it all, from an artistic standpoint?"

"I think it stinks. If it keeps up I'm going to have to move."

"What?"

"Beachful of stupid bastards all the time. Don't they have homes? Run you down on the highways."

"What?"

"Goddamn tourists are bad enough one season a year without having them all year around."

"Agh."

"It used to be beautiful down here and free, like pelicans," Tipton said. "A man could walk up and down. Now fifty million houses and things. God, I hate to see it. My heart hurts about it."

"Are you by any chance joking, Mr. Tipton?" Space asked stiffly.

"Call me Cliff. Joking hell. I can't even sleep on the beach any more for polka-dot halters. I had a good friend, a retired Irishman—not that he left the Church—who went into bootlegging and did well. But he moved, just the other year, because he couldn't swim naked at Blackjack Cove any more. Said no place you can't swim naked in is worth it. He's right."

"Well," said Space, arising. "I had no idea."

"Ruined the fishing too, I understand. What the hell is Florida for if you can't sleep in it? People racing up and down the road honking. What is Florida for if you can't keep some little son of a bitch from Chicago from running you over in a motorboat?"

"Mr. Tipton, I'm afraid—"

"Oh, it's all right for you," Cliff said conversationally. "You make your living off other people and you don't have much fun anyhow. But from an artistic standpoint, like you said, I have thought this out carefully. To hell with progress."

Rick seemed to be waiting for the thunder to crack the heavens. But the only sound was Tipton eating his ice cubes.

Space's face was cold as he looked down and said, "Terribly sorry to have taken up your time, Mr. Tipton. Now, if you will excuse me."

"Sure."

As Space and Rick walked away to the sound of muffled and ominous drums, Trudy Tipton, whose instincts approached telepathy, walked over, looked down at her husband and said, "I take it you've worn out our welcome?"

"Look at the seat of his pants. Soaking wet."

"Well, let's go. Did you notice how nice the moon is tonight?"

"Romantic. It's a shame we're married."

Mrs. Tipton told Mrs. Space what a nice evening it had been. When she got to the car Cliff was holding the schnapps bottle up to the moonlight. One swallow.

"Hey," he said. "Wait. I'll be right back."

He walked back to the party area and, picking up a handful of shrimp, asked Rick, "What *is* a weather ball?"

"A large aluminum affair," Rick said, coldly. "It shows green when no temperature change is expected, it shows red for warm and blue for cooler. It is some ten feet in diameter and visible at night up to twelve miles. When rain is predicted it flashes off and on in the color of the temperature trend expected to accompany the precipitation."

"Well, I'll be," said Cliff Tipton, and went home.

The following editorial appeared in all Space newspapers throughout Florida a few days later, in early March:

"BOOST, DON'T KNOCK!

"The eyes of this mighty nation remain glued on Florida.

"The dynamic growth of this state amazes all and sundry. It is our modest hope that we have in some small way, we of Space Publications, Inc., contributed to that growth—a growth we hope to symbolize in that lofty spire of soon-to-be-completed Progress Tower, an erection pointing to the soft blue skies of the Sunshine State.

"This being our view and our firm editorial stand, a stand definitely for Progress in all its many manifestations, we were saddened recently to learn the views of a prominent writer who resides in this lovely land we call Florida.

"We shall not name him. Perhaps he may yet recant. We

shall only say it is with sorrow and a tinge of regret we learn of his outlook—he, who could be such a powerful propagandist for this nature's wonderland.

"Yes, we were even shocked to hear him flatly state he resented —actually resented!—the influx of our neighbors from the North, the happy people who, by the unnumbered thousands, are deserting the snow and slush of the Northland to discover a fabulous new life in Florida.

"We were shocked to hear him say he actually resented the happy vacationers, as well as the permanent newcomers, who in increasing numbers and on an increasingly year-round basis are availing themselves of the pleasures in this golden state.

"Yes, and most of all we were shocked to hear him say he actually planned to move because of these wondrous happenings; we were shocked and saddened.

"Withal, however, perhaps it would be the best thing for this misguided individual who would stand in the path of Progress. Perhaps he should move, move from this beauteous land wherein he has dwelled and profited most greatly.

"Perhaps he should become a hermit, find some isolated place to live, far from the dynamic sounds of growth and the happy cries of people in this perpetual vacationland.

"Yes, that may well be the answer. Nothing will halt this march. The anti-social, the Red, the crooked labor leader, the misanthrope must remember that the Bright and Shiny Bulldozer of Progress is the voice of the future. They must move from the path of the Shiny Bulldozer or be trampled underfoot like a straw in the wind! Get out or get on the bandwagon!

"For—and mark this well—progresswise, we shall continue to advance!!!"

This editorial was read by John Riley of Riley Real Estate in a small beach cottage at the Surfside-Sands at Guava Springs. He was seated in an easy chair, scanning the papers. His newest secretary was sitting up in bed, combing her hair and humming tunelessly; occasionally snapping her gum.

She was a shapely girl even with her clothes on, which was not now the case save for a shortie nightie which gave her the look of Salome in The semi-final veil. Unfortunately, she was amazingly stupid and Riley detested trying to communicate with her verbally. She was under strict orders not to talk at all, and he always carried reading material with him to the cottage.

This worked out nicely, for she was content to brush her hair for hours, or perhaps days, on end while staring into space in friendly fashion. Meanwhile he caught up on events of the day.

"Profited greatly."

These words leaped out at Riley, who was interested in profit. He read the entire editorial and chuckled. Must be that character Cliff Tipton, he thought. Boy, he thought, that guy hit the jackpot.

Suddenly, Riley's mind whipped back and forth like a cash register drawer. Tipton planning to move? Wanted solitude? Out of the past came remembrance of a gold bathtub of another character who wanted solitude—and found it in south central Florida. By damn, thought John Riley excitedly, if I play my cards right I bet I can unload the old Space place on him! The fact he didn't own it, and wasn't quite sure who did, bothered him not one bit—for he was a real estate man.

"Hey," he said to the girl in bed. "Can you take shorthand?"

"Take what, Johnny?"

A few mornings after the editorial appeared, an inspirational message arrived at the office of Harrington Space, from Clifton Tipton.

Harrington read the inspirational message with great gratification. Why, he thought happily, I changed Cliff's mind. The power of the press is staggering!

He thought the message was just the thing. He called his key men and asked what they thought. They said they thought it was just the thing.

He asked his son what he thought.

Jerry was learning the key man end of the business.

Jerry read it slowly and said, "Just the thing. I never saw anything just the thinger."

In gratitude Harrington Space sent Cliff Tipton a boat, a runabout. Tipton later wrecked it in collision with a wholesale shoe distributor from New York City.

The message approved for chiseling into Progress Tower read:

> PROGRESS . . .
> Progress . . .
> Without progress there
> Can be
> No advancement . . .
>
> Progress?
> Forward! For to progress one
> Must inevitably move
> Forward, else lose the name
> Of Progress . . .
>
> Progress!
> Nor faintly query how!
> By sharp prow
> Forward and with stern
> Arear—well tillered . . .
>
> Progress,
> Ahead. And with full-throated
> Cry, sharp as this lofty and speared
> Spire, pointing the sun,
> All hail the forwardness of
> PROGRESS!

CHAPTER FIVE

IT HAD BEEN A STULTIFYING day at Creation, Ltd., another "conference" day wherein men sat around a table proving, still *again* how smart they were, and Paul Higgins was scowling a little as he walked his accustomed path through the streets of the thronging city in the early, twinkling evening of New York.

Paul did not look forward to the commuter bit—and everything was a "bit" no matter how hard you tried not to pick up the jargon from the James A. Wedleys—and he did not look forward to the morrow. He walked fast, with his hands jammed deep in his pockets, his hat pushed back on the thick gray-black hair, ennui deep in his soul and the frown on his brow like a smudge, turning his head a little from side to side, watching the people come by. A man in a brown Homburg, with a complaining face and moving lips, was tattling to his angels. A mean-faced girl waited for a poodle to urinate. *Click!* the stop lights went.

All the cities I have walked through, Paul thought, taking his long fast strides, his thick shoulders swaying; how different all of them were. And how different must be the ones I didn't see. I wonder if they miss me?

But it was March now and the air was fresh and cool with the smell of waiting spring and New York City was all around him, and that meant quite a bit he supposed. Paul looked at the city as he walked through it, toward the station; looked up at the lights flickering impatiently for dark and fulfillment and he looked, turning his head to watch it go, at a blowing newspaper skittering.

("His idea of art, see," Paul once had overheard a ferret-faced man say to a lynx-faced man at Groson's, the place where media men go, "is a long shot of this newspaper blowing down this street at dawn. Now he likes this, O.K. I like this, O.K. You like this, O.K. But will the sponsor like this? So, we get ourselves another boy, eh?")

Thusly, Paul walked down the sidewalk, toward where it comes to a point, and he turned, thus; walked the correct number of blocks and turned left.

For this is the way she goes, Paul thought, this is the way she goes.

But I have Job Security and a Fine Home, and there are really no more cities to go to—except Paris, perhaps, which, he thought, I fully intended to make, although I will not go to Paris this month—no—and look at upturned eyes. I will not go next month, either. For I have a dentist's appointment; one must watch the tartar, the unctuous dentist quoth. So here we go down the street in March.

How did Indian braves feel, he wondered, walking through the tall quiet trees?

Young Indians or forty-five-year-old Indians?

Any goddamn Indians!

He went into the station and got on his commuters' train. Here I go with the rest of them, he thought, through the early evening, on a train I will ride until when? But that is the way she goes, my boy, that is the way she goes.

His hands and face were blunt. He had been a cynic until nearly thirty. Now his eyes weren't sure. His face, profiled against the train window, was weary but stubborn. As a younger man he had been given to explosive temper, which is a disease, like alcoholism, but he had whipped it (for the most part) by clenching and bunching his jaw muscles. People said he was a slow man to know, but only the people who did not know him.

When the train reached his station he moved down the aisle easy as an Indian, moved through the rest of them, making the tribal grunts, and swung down on the platform. It was a four-teen-block walk to his home and he walked it because golf bored him.

The day had left the green-copper taste of irritation in his mouth. There had been too many telephones, too much Wedley. Paul hated telephones. Art Rodes loved telephones. Telephones were to Art as cathedrals were to some others; they brought him peace and tranquility.

To Art, the idea of speaking softly into a telephone (action) and causing something to move in a predetermined direction (reaction) was—balm. Some men play with electric trains as Art Rodes played with telephones.

Right now Art would be at Groson's with the big-eyed and brunette and out-of-town niece of a client, Paul reflected.

"Mr. Rodes, tell me. Exactly what does a public relations man do?"

"My dear, I am rather taken aback at the penetrating intelligence of your question, so unusual in one so young. Move around here—let me diagram this for you. My, your drink is empty."

The no-good son of a bitch, Paul thought, walking down the suburban street, grinning a little.

Neither man had ever quite figured out the other one. They had known each other for twenty years. Once they had worked together in Little Rock on a paper; briefly, in passing, they had been on the same paper in Atlanta. Without seeming to, or even on purpose, they kept in touch. Each had recognized the other.

Paul stayed in the newspaper business a long time and considered it a profession.

Art had considered it a stepping stone and, offered a public relations job in his twenties, had dropped newspapering like an empty bottle.

At the end of World War II Rode was making $17,500 a year while Higgins, discharged from the Air Corps, considered himself lucky to be on a New York rewrite desk at not quite $100 a week. In those years he was going to be a writer and wrote short stories on the side and sold some of them at good rates.

In those years, each man was a comer. Art Rodes became an account executive. People could tell a Higgins story in the paper even without a byline. Rodes was lured to Creation, Ltd., for a $1,500 raise. Paul rose to $115 a week.

"Come in with us," Rodes said to Paul. "Otto wants you."

"No. It's not for me."

"Come in with us," Art said, six months later, and named the price.

"Paul, it's your decision," said Betty Higgins. "You'll do all right either way. But it's your decision."

Paul at that time had a little girl and another child on the way. He lived in a walk-up apartment. He went to a department store in late December to charge a leather coat for Betty's present—she had always wanted a leather coat—and a slip came down in the chute telling him to report to the eighth floor, credit department, to discuss his account. He got a little lecture and the thin-faced man said, "Well, I *guess* we can let you have the coat but please keep your payments up to date."

He was the top writer in his shop, or one of them, but it didn't seem to mean much.

"Maybe in public relations I'll have more time for outside writing," he said to his wife.

"Sure you will," said Art Rodes. "Put away that sherry. I brought some scotch."

"Good luck," said the city editor when he left.

He had cleaned his desk out for the next man; you do that. He walked out of the newspaper business with two half-finished short stories, a peanut butter glass he kept his pencils in and two new typewriter ribbons he was stealing for his portable. The man who replaced him considered "journalism" a stepping stone.

"What the hell does a public relations man do, Art?"

"Well, let's take it from the basic, Paul."

"Once on a small paper I doubled in advertising. As I remember, all the local merchants wanted their ads to say: 'JUST ARRIVED, NEW SHIPMENT. BEAN PLANTS, SHEEP MANURE. U SAVE HERE.'"

"Exactly," Art said. "Exactly."

It had been quite a few years now since Paul had worried about bills. He had money. He had stocks. He had a nice home. He had savings. He told himself, at forty-five, that he didn't know how lucky he was. It had been five years since he had finished a story, three years since he quit working frequently on his book.

He guessed maybe he wasn't going to be a writer after all.

"What's gnawing you, Paul?" Art had asked one day. "You don't miss the newspaper business, do you, at this late date?"

"No. I never did. I was there already."

"The place you miss is where you never been?" Art had asked.

"I got to get this survey under way, Art."

Otto Anvel had once asked, "What makes you and Art such a good team, Paul?"

Paul said: "He knows what public relations men do right. I know what they do wrong. What else is there?"

"Nothing. Are you planning to leave me, Paul?"

"Where would I go?"

Go? Paul thought, walking toward his home in the soft night. Why, I don't know how lucky I am.

His home, a nice house, glowed in the dark. He went in. His daughter deigned to smile brightly at him from the sofa. Jamison somebody also smiled brightly. Jamison had intellectual bangs like a twisted-motivation-type writer.

Another boy, and a pony-tail girl, were seated cross-legged on the living room rug, the girl showing entirely too much inner thigh. Obviously they were doing something intellectual so Paul went on into the kitchen.

That Jamison, he thought, has got a head like a cantaloupe with fringe on it.

Too *much* thigh? he remembered suddenly. Boy! You are getting up there. Just the other day, driving from home to the liquor store on a Saturday afternoon, he had espied the rear view of a voluptuous lassie in tight-tight shorts and in the midst of his carnal thoughts—he had rolled them down about knee level in his mind's eye—recognized the girl as a friend of Lou's since the fourth grade, and immediately felt like a child molester apprehended at a girl scout picnic. A victim of mixed emotions.

"How do you find the diameter of a circle?" asked Paul Higgins, Junior, who was doing his homework on the kitchen table. He was a dark-eyed boy with a short nose and a square face and cynical eyebrows.

"Why?" said Paul. "Is one missing?"

"How *do* you?"

"Hold a ruler across that thick part of it and measure it," said his father. "However, if you mean how do you find the circumference of a circle, ask your mother. Where is your mother?"

"Emptying the garbage. Which is the radius?"

"Hello," said Betty Higgins, coming into the kitchen lugging a red plastic garbage can. "Drink?"

"I'll get them. Hello." He kissed her.

From the living room, Jamison, tossing his fringe, said loudly, "Well, Perry Mae, regardless of what you say I believe it has been pretty well agreed that the Proustian scalpel is far superior to the blunt and obvious axe blade of—"

"Double goddamn," muttered Paul.

"*Paul!*" Betty hissed, looking at their son.

"He can't hear me inside that circle. Let's sit outside."

They sat on the back steps.

"Louise called today, Paul."

"Louise who?"

"Your sister-in-law, stupid. My sister, Louise."

"Called from Florida?"

"From Guava Springs. She wants us to buy a house in Florida."

"She wants *everybody* to buy a house in Florida."

"She said this was different."

"Did you tell her we already had a house in New York and Florida is a little too far to commute to New York 17?"

"She seemed so excited. She's going to write about it. Something she overheard—a real shrewdie type deal, a sleeper, she said. A wonderful investment."

"You have garbage on your nose."

From the living room Jamison screeched: "Thomas Wolfe? Oh, Lou, my dear, I mean after all! How *could* you?"

"Someday," Paul gritted, yanking the back door shut, "I am going to peel that repulsive little mutt like a Bermuda onion."

"Louise said it would be a wonderful buy, and she's pretty smart, my sister."

(Louise had always been after him to move to Florida, Paul thought. "If you're going to be a writer," she had said, "get down here and write." The past few years it had rankled.)

Paul said, "You sound like you want to go."

Betty said: "I thought maybe for vacations. Or just an investment."

"Don't lie."

"All right. I'm tired of watching you clamber aboard a train toward a job you don't like, every morning."

"I do so like it. It's a good job. What would you have me do? Starve?"

"We've got money. Quite a bit."

"Oh, Jesus Christ."

"Look, you," Betty Higgins said, standing up, abruptly. "I don't give a happy damn whether you work for Otto Anvel or for the World-Telegram or for the Fuller Brush Company or wherever—but you better quit being halfway about it. I can't be happy when you aren't."

"Maybe when Lou is through college. I can't pull out now. Hell, I'm no kid."

"Paul, Paul."

"This is the route we chose, kid."

"Then make up your mind."

"Let's eat," he said. "I'm going to do some work tonight."

"On the story?"

"On the book. Hell, honey, there's no reason I can't do it right here. And ride the old gravy train too."

They had dinner, then brandy, then talked a while. He never carried a briefcase, but he brought his work home with him in his head. He decided to wait until his mind was clearer to work on the book. And he went to bed fairly early. He had had a hard day.

Over Slathesdale, N.Y., the half moon lay on its back, pale and sallow.

At midnight Peter Patzy Pomerelo walked into Groson's, his eyes speculative, his little pink-rimmed eyes which brightened when they focused on Arthur Rodes, he of the easy touch, he of the beautiful bountifulness, and to Arthur Rodes, Peter Patzy Pomerelo said, "Buy you a drink, boy?"

"How much?" asked Art, grinning.

"Oh, you are a grand and perceptive man. A hundred. But I will settle for fifty."

From his $-shaped money clip Art peeled seventy-five dollars and handed them to P. P. Pomerelo, who smiled, and paid for the drinks, and left a dollar tip and went out into the night to seek his fortune.

The bartender said to Art, "I would not lend that grifter a dime with a dollar as collateral."

"And you should not. The only kind of person Pete would ever pay back is the kind who would lend to him. Remember that."

"I'm trying to forget it. What does it mean?"

"Hell, I don't know. Yes I do. It means it takes one to know one. Not what you're thinking, Bert."

Arthur Rodes, then, went outside into the night, walking the deck, feeling the dark and smiling, the long thin cigar between his teeth, the aliveness known within him—aha, aha! he thought, New York on a night like this: The biggest show, the greatest city, the most unpredictable place ever devised by mortal man, a place to make Olympus look from Cubesville— Babylon sticks up real noplace. And here I am, he thought, right by-damn here in the middle of it.

He laughed. A doorman laughed back, for the doorman also liked the night, and had hit a three-horse parlay, and been given the lowered eyelids by the young wife of the old broker upstairs, and understood that money wasn't everything, and felt tonight in his epaulets like an admiral, instead of like a damn fool.

The doorman was laughing as Art Rodes pushed his hat down over his eyes, like the vaudeville men, and strode purposefully, aimlessly, nodding to people and occasionally talking to the inhabitants of the night.

All very good and funny tonight.

For I am a public relations man, he told himself solemnly and doubled up inside to keep from laughing aloud. ("Well, you're more one hell of a good private relations man, I'll tell you that, buster," the brunette niece had said.)

If anybody in the entire, wide universe enjoyed *being* their profession, their art, it was Rodes, the public relations man incarnate.

He felt like calling somebody up.

His hand was hungry for the voluptuous smoothness of a telephone. He had never felt more alive.

He walked faster and faster, wanting to drink, wanting to talk, not lonely although he had neither chick nor child.

"Hagh!" he said, suddenly, as the pain gripped his chest. *What was that?*

The pain in his shoulder was not good. He knew all about heart attacks. Life had done a piece, and so had many others. He thought for a minute he was having a heart attack.

But, he thought, I have no fear—you're supposed to have this terrible fear. As he was looking for the fear, the pain ceased. He had not even quit grinning, although it had hurt.

"Must have been a bad clam," they said at Bleeck's.

He told the local joke about the reporter's dream-story which ends with the telephone ringing in the middle of the night and the reporter answering and this voice saying, "Hello. This is Judge Crater. Where did everybody go?"

Later—the middle of one day—he learned what pain was.

CHAPTER SIX

THE SPACE PLACE SAT IN ITS silent grove far from the busy world, and down on the deep black lake the musing ripples moved.

A small alligator in the cypress knees without malice ate up a gar.

The moon was yellow and getting orange as the month got older and riper, the month of March. Peace is the color of a dark blue night and Flat County had dark blue it hadn't used yet.

The old house sat in the mossy trees, refusing to lease to ghosts. It was far from dead, not even dying; merely waiting for somebody to come.

A shutter slapped and a hinge snapped and the wind blew all around easily. Florida stretched out like a puddled prairie, a thumb of palmettoed sand in patient seas.

The edges of Florida were bright-lighted and frantic but the interior was the soft dark blue, down south. A tomato princeling

in a Ford station wagon handed his lady the pint of Seagrams-7.
She drank contentedly, got back into the front seat and the
headlights poked at the darkness of Flat County, then the darkness closed in again. Peace was here in Flat County.

Peace was there, much peace. And John Riley, in Guava
Springs, thought he knew where he could sell it.

Visions of profit were dancing in his head. Last week Riley
had checked it out. This was mid-March. The old Space place
still stood unoccupied and still owned by the holding company
used by Harrington Space, Riley had found, and could be
bought cheap.

Of course he wouldn't actually buy it until he sold it first, so
to speak—for John Riley was, while a romanticist, an eminently
practical man. One hooks the sucker first—one does not get
stuck with a bucket of stale bait.

That was all the ancient alchemists sought, that combination,
and John Riley, the real estate man, had long since caught up
on his car payments—a carrot-donkey race he had always lost
when working for Space publications. Now he drove a Lincoln.

A romanticist was John Riley the Real Estate Man. He had
been a terrible real estate editor but a fine romanticist; he had
the soul of a minor poet and once he got out of the newspaper
business into the real estate business where creative ability
counts for something, this poetic bent had proven an asset instead of a liability.

Riley's mind, like the mind of any good poet, moved like
the gears in a slot machine.

If Tipton was disgusted with the new Florida, why, simply
sell him a bit of the old.

He had run into minor difficulties in locating Tipton immediately after reading the editorial. Tipton's wife said he was
attending the funeral of the sales manager of a graveyard-plot
organization. Riley had not been easily put off, and kept trying.

John Riley had a poetic soul; he had also the brain of a major
gypsy horse trader and money had not dulled him. A deal was

still a deal. He did not sell the steak, he sold the gristle. A profitable deal was a profitable deal and the thrill to John Riley was still as great as in his early and immediately post-virginial days, for Riley was a Florida Real Estate Man, a throwback to the old breed, a man who had sat at the half-soled feet of the old Boca Raton masters—Riley had seen those half soles turn to calfskin, and Riley had been inspired: John Riley, his round red face shining and blithe, was a promise of things *even yet to come* in the Sunshine State.

For he was a real estate man, procurer and purveyor of God's Green Acres, measuring the earth with a footrule and taking the measure of man with a sidelong glance.

A very good real estate man was he.

As were his many peers.

They have seen the brackish bays where sewage washed and where jellyfish were thick. "I'll buy it, here's the binder," they have said, and they filled it in and created brochures and spoke of it in the market place and sold it (gleefully) and mansions stand now on the shore and, dolefully, they say they should have held on to that property; would be a rich man today. They have seen the sandspur flats where the ground rattler mused and where the atmosphere was bleak. I can *sell* that, they thought, taking the option, and the stately *jai alai* court makes merry the night, the dog race track is crowded, the pizzaburger seeketh its mate.

On the far-flung keys where were rickety bridges and where only lived a hermit of independent WPA wealth—even here they have envisioned the potentialities and they have said to others of the race of men, owners of these places: "While we're not at all sure it's worth our time and trouble, perhaps you can work out something which will be mutually satisfactory."

They are *real estate men*, down there on the thumb, and their equal has not been elsewhere seen.

The bulldozers roam and the draglines strain and the black glass brick arises.

They are real estate men, real estate men! and their voices are as melodic as a well-tuned lute, their sport shirts as gay as pennants on a gasparilla sloop, their hands expressive and their vision keen. Meekness is not their weapon. They seek not to inherit the earth; they only want a damn good commission on its turnover.

"Where's my other sock?" John Riley had demanded that first morning he read the editorial, and his secretary, a good sock finder but weak on shorthand, had found it. He had jumped into his yellow convertible and down the asphalt roared.

He rushed into the nearest open lounge, the Sandsides, and telephoned the Tipton home. That was the day he was told Mr. Tipton was at the funeral. Riley sat there at the bar, drumming his fingers, a short, stocky man with a crimson face and a yellow sports shirt with little green fish on it.

I'll find him, he thought. I'll hook that Tipton.

Something kept bothering him.

Oops, he thought, snapping his fingers and chuckling. Left my secretary at the motel.

The next few days Riley pursued Tipton with no success. But he didn't give up. Like any good no-limit player he waited for a good run of the cards.

Also, like any other no-limit player, he had one flaw. His particular flaw was that he talked too much.

Nature is against monopoly, creation has its own antitrust laws. Else John Riley, or a spiritual brother, would own us all.

He talked too much. That one gear in his head was flawed. After hours of talking business, exercising his vision, he still felt the need to talk. He could not talk to his wife, because she understood him. His secretary was barely capable of coherent speech. Who he talked to was his office manager, Miss Murdine.

Miss Murdine was sixty. She wore rimless glasses over utterly objective eyes. Neither cruelty nor compassion had ever come to live in Miss Murdine. She was emotionless. She took things as they came. Her sole addiction was cigarettes in a filter holder. Occasionally she took a lemon drop. She was an excellent office manager. All the figures were right where they belonged.

Miss Murdine would never have violated a confidence. John Riley spilled the beans all by himself.

"Coffee's on me, girls!" John Riley boomed one morning, shoving into the booth with Miss Murdine and her friend, Louise Antel, who ran the Coffee Shop.

Happily, he told Miss Murdine all about his scheme to hook Cliff Tipton. That Louise Antel was listening, he did not consider. People never think people who own places are listening. John Riley told how shrewd he was, how the place was available for a song, how he was going to make his pitch to Tipton—when he found him—and how he would pick up a whopping profit.

"The land alone is worth what they're asking," Riley said. "I might even buy the place even if I can't sell Tipton."

"You really think it's such a good investment?" asked Louise Antel, whose late husband had been an investment broker.

"Sure is," said Riley. "You bet!"

"Is it?" Louise asked Miss Murdine.

Miss Murdine nodded yes.

The next day Louise didn't open her shop. She drove to Flat County. She looked at the Space place, smiled slightly and drove back to Guava Springs. She had felt the soil, looked at the sky, picked a mango and considered the lake and river.

Louise had called her sister Betty in New York. She worried about her younger sister, to some extent. She had seen how her sister lived. She had seen what had happened to Paul Higgins. She had known Paul for twenty-one years and remembered when his hatbrim was turned up and when Betty thought he was all romance.

She had known Paul when he had an ambition large enough for him.

She did not want her sister to live with a shriveling man.

Louise, herself, had married a careful-eyed man who looked dry and precise but who took her to Florida and freedom and feared no reasonable risk and had never been afraid until the day he died, or that day either.

Betty had married a writer who looked wild and romantic but who had quit writing to choose a sure bet and who took her to a hemmed-in rich Yankee suburb and who spent three hours a day dying fretfully on a train, trying to rationalize.

And only talked about writing and drank too much.

You have to drink too much up there, thought Louise, driving back across the flat peninsula.

"Anyhow," she said to her sister on the phone, that mid-March afternoon, "tell Paul if he really wants out, it's down here for him. Very good investment. Matter of fact, tell him for me to put up or shut up—he's beginning to make me tired."

Old Louise, Paul thought that night, after Betty told him about the call, trying to sleep. A great gal. I used to think she was dry as sawdust. I used to think that little man she was married to was a walking cipher. I used to think lots of things.

My wife, he thought, worries about me.

He counted the money he had in the bank.

He counted sheep, he counted clients, he counted years, he got up and lit a cigarette. Blank copy paper was in the typewriter and the sallow moonlight fell on it.

He looked out on the adequately zoned street.

"Are you asleep, Betty?"

He felt his middle through his pajamas. There was some suet there.

Forty-five, fifty, fifty-five, sixty. Sixty-five?

He was far from sure about anything. This was a great disadvantage to him.

CHAPTER SEVEN

IF A PROSAIC PLODDER LIKE Higgins can make it, then *I* certainly can, James A. Wedley thought positively. He jutted his jaw, standing there in the office in his shirt sleeves. He let his left eyebrow rise. Miss Mason, a copywriter with red hair, was watching him, he knew, and he exhaled a stream of smoke, decisively as if the frosted-glass door already said J. Aaron Wedley.

He waited until Higgins left Rodes' office because he hated to have Higgins see his creative work. Higgins, thought James A., has the imagination of a plowhorse. He has the mind of a newspaperman, scornfully thought James A., who had worked on the Princeton paper but left that sort of thing behind with other juvenile pursuits.

Wedley had often been sorely wounded by Higgins, but Rodes was different. Rodes *got* things.

Wedley's sleeves were rolled up. He had on suspenders. By golly, he thought, I *look* like an account executive already.

(Some of the others were watching now: The pony-tail with the strand loose over one eye, the brisk girl who never sat down but was always carrying things, the copy chief, they were all watching.)

Typewriters were the orchestration in the workshop of Creation, Ltd., which moulded public opinion. James A. Wedley, who carried briefcases in elevators, moved across the room. Miss Mason, red-haired, who is fragrant and who looks straight ahead in the elevators in New York, watched him go, go through the frosted-glass door, high up in the great city where by pluck and perseverance even a Princeton man may scale the heights of success.

"Well," said James A. to Art, "This is the crop. At least, it reflects the highlights. I'd like to get the benefit of your thinking."

Art Rodes never admitted the existence of hangovers. It was perhaps his nearest thing to a true spiritual quality. This morning he was a trifle shaky in his faith but it didn't show. He clamped down on the thin cigar, like biting a bullet, and he looked up with his narrow eyes, brightly as an eagle scout after a bracing dip. He scanned the reflections of the highlights. When he looked directly at James A. his eyes were the eyes of Blackbeard admiring the daring of a subordinate buccaneer.

"Jimmy boy," he said, "you're off and running."

"Whew," said Wedley, sitting down, stretching his legs, a genius exhausted. "You don't think it's, well, too much?"

"It's so much too much it underplays," said Art. "It comes around for the second time and evens up. It gyroscopes. You can hear it hum."

"I'm glad to hear you say that. Gyroscopes, eh?"

"I—uh."

With the pain the terror came to Arthur Rodes who thought he would die now.

"My God," breathed Wedley and screamed for Higgins as Art went sideways slowly out of the chair, face contorted.

He's only forty-eight, Paul thought in the ambulance on the way to the hospital. *It reaches out and gets you wherever you are.*

At the hospital they took Art's cart away fast and Paul sat waiting. He will be dead, Paul thought. Dr. Hills said he was not dead.

"How bad?"

"We don't know yet."

The doctor said what doctors say. Wait and see.

Paul saw the woman at the information desk, she was disheveled and frantic, twisting at her purse strap with near hysteria. "I'm sorry," the poker-faced woman at the information desk kept saying with a voice like a telephone operator. "There is no Paul Higgins here. You must have the wrong hospital, Madam."

"Betty!" Paul said.

"Oh, my God, my God!" she cried.

He held her.

"They called. They said it was you. Maybe they didn't."

"No. It was Art. I told the switchboard to tell you I had gone with Art. That stupid bitch on the switchboard."

"Maybe I misunderstood. I thought it was you. How is he? Oh, God, Paul, I thought it was you. How *is* he?"

"We don't know yet, Mrs. Higgins," Dr. Hills said. "Wait and see."

Paul said, "Are you all right?"

"Yes."

But outside she swayed and almost fell. "I cursed the poor taxi driver," she sobbed. "For going so slow."

"Easy, easy."

"It *could* have been you."

"Shhh."

"Will he die?"

In the bar down the street they sat together and held hands silently. The blood came back to her lips and before long her hand was warm again. He thought of the many times he had held it.

"I thought it was all over," she said. "I thought, what a waste. I thought you were gone, gone."

"Shhh."

"Before it *is* you," she said, then, "we better go be happy."

"Yes."

"This would be such a futile way to die."

"Yes it would."

"Then we'll go, won't we?"

"Yes, Betty."

Through the city toward the bridge they started the long ride home. The lights were bright and a siren wailed and millions of people carried their thoughts in their heads. Nobody ever knows what he will do, Paul thought; ever in this world. Now I will leave this city, and already I am late.

At home, Betty called her sister and said she was flying down. To look at the house. Next Thursday, April third.

Betty had called for the reservation before calling her sister.

"You couldn't make a better investment," Louise Antel said. "Honey, have you been crying or do we have a bad connection?"

CHAPTER EIGHT

M<small>R. AND MRS. AL HOLTMAN AND</small> Mr. and Mrs. Ricky Rollero were lying on the sand of the private beach at the Siesta Surfside on Guava Springs Key, listening to a portable radio and watching a thin, brown, elderly man surf-fishing. He was waist deep in the Gulf, casting easily with his heavy rod. Outlined against the sunset he looked like a retirement ad for an insurance company.

The Holtmans and the Rolleros were Northern Visitors. They were visiting Guava Springs Key for the first time. They had heard the West Coast was the place, even better than Miami.

They and their fellow tourists were viewed with delight by the progressive-minded elements among the locals, and particularly by the Space newspapers, which termed them "our neighbors from the Northland who come to observe and who go back home as goodwill ambassadors for the Sunshine State, determined to seek out the good life in Florida upon retirement or, and in increasing numbers, during their active, productive years."

"I got a gutfulla this joint," said Mr. Holtman to Mr. Rollero.

"Yeh," said Mr. Rollero to Mr. Holtman. "I wanted to go back to Miami this year like any sanity type, but the old lady drags me here."

"Yeh."

Mr. Holtman was lean and in topcoats in Detroit and Mr. Rollero was plump and in used automobiles in Cleveland. They were listening to news from the leased wires of the Associated Press. Mrs. Holtman and Mrs. Rollero were discussing the sunset.

"Like I was telling Ricky just last night you could sit a million years in Cleveland without ever seeing like this over the ocean." Mrs. Rollero said, scratching.

"I love nature. Al complains about the heat but I just love nature."

"Look, so many colors."

Mrs. Holtman was quite chubby and wore flared pink shorts and a polka-dot halter and on her feet were raffia sandals. Mr. Holtman had on a wide Mexican straw hat, Lastex trunks, a bright yellow terrycloth shirt and a corn plaster. Mr. Rollero wore a long-billed cap, purple trunks, purple sport shirt and smoked a thick black cigar. Mrs. Rollero had on harlequin sunglasses, bright red clam-diggers so tight she had to tug at them surreptitiously on occasion, and a pair of low-quartered, crimson sneakers. They had taken pictures of each other earlier.

The radio stated: "This is Montgomery Jones, signing off with this thought—hope may spring eternal but at the same time it quite often is always darkest before the disaster. A good evening to you all—and good Murrow. I mean morror." Then the radio inquired: "Friends. Are you sure of your brake lining?"

Up and down the beaches, all around the coast of the peninsula, the radios had said the evening news. The night could arrive now.

"It looks pretty bad," said Mr. Holtman.

"They better do something," said Mr. Rollero.

The straight, tan, old man in the khaki shorts was emerging from the water, the casting rod at right shoulder.

"Any luck?" asked Mr. Rollero.

The old man looked at them and did not exactly smile. He shook his head from side to side, thoughtfully. He scratched his great shock of white hair and he said, "Nope. Makes no difference. Just out for my health."

"Hah!" said Al Holtman. "Health! This place is killing me. Damn sun. Salt, sand fleas, flies. A lizard was in the glove compartment. I told that woman, but no. No."

"This place has been healthful for me," the old man said. "Couldn't even walk when I got here."

"Really?" said Mrs. Holtman, curious even though she sensed the man was a social inferior. She knew that intuitively.

"Was flat on my back," the old man said. "Couldn't even feed myself. Weighed next to nothing. Had to be taken care of round the clock."

"Amazing," said Mr. Holtman.

"Even grew a good stand of hair down here. Had been bald as a doorknob. Had no power of speech when I got here. Could hardly communicate. Couldn't stand up. No control over my bodily functions. Well, so long, folks."

"Hey," Rollero called, as the old man strolled off down the beach. "How long you lived in Florida?"

"Seventy-three years," he called. "Born here."

"Smartass cracker bastard," Holtman muttered.

"They'll take you for everything you've got," Rollero said.

"What I would like, Ricky, is a good, cold, drinky-winky with lots of gin in it."

Back to their respective cottages they went in the soft swift twilight; shaved, showered and left in Rollero's station wagon, roaring down the blacktop road, past the Spray-Spa, past the Bide-a-Tide, to the air-conditioned bar they liked. It was as gloomy as the better lounges back home. A big juke organ spewed softly insane color. A big man was sitting on the end stool at the bar, eyeing the juke organ curiously and eating ice cubes.

The foursome came in and passed him. The girls had changed to pedal pushers and bright blouses and clogs. The men had on other-colored shirts and shorts. Mrs. Rollero pulled delicately at the rear of her pedal pushers. Mrs. Holtman wore her rhinestone sun glasses in the dark. The Seaside was packed with the cocktail hour crowd.

"Lots of famous people live on Guava Springs Key," Mrs. Rollero said, to Mrs. Holtman.

"It has the reputation of being real cultural."

"I was telling Al—" said Mrs. Holtman. "Hey! There's one now!" She peered through her sun glasses.

"Where? Where?"

"The one chewing gum. I seen his picture in the Free Press. The writer. What's his name, Tipton. You know, wrote the book about the typical town with all the, you know, sex in it."

"Was it a movie?"

"Not yet."

"I didn't read it. I like to wait until they come out in the movies because otherwise you read it the book spoils the ending sometimes."

"Yeh, I know. Anyhow, I seen his picture all over."

"That's not gum. That's ice cubes."

"I saw Myrna Loy in an airplane I was in when I was flying to stay with my sister at Long Beach when she was having her gall bladder, rather gallstones, out."

"You want to get his autograph?"

"My husband would raise a objection. He's so what you call withdrawn."

"So's mine."

"Yee-AYY!" the juke organ shouted suddenly and Cliff
Tipton spilled his drink. "Yec-AY! Be my little panda bear and
I will take you everywhere, yee-AY! We will make a steady
loving pair because baby you're no square. Yee-AY!"

The singer was accompanying himself on the electric guitar.

"You're a cutie say you're a doll, I love you long and I love
you tall, nobody'll loveya like I love you, you're a blue-jean
hipster and my love is true-blue. Yee-AY!"

"What is that?" Tipton's voice was controlled. "Tell me
please, Bert."

The bartender walked over and studied the titles.

"Yee-AY, Mr. Tipton."

"Skol, Bert."

Well, where is the dumb son of a bitch? Cliff wondered,
looking around the bar. Damn if I'll wait on him much longer
even if I don't know him. John Riley? John Riley? Now why
would I agree to make an appointment and meet a John Riley?
Who is John Riley, what is he? John Riley. John Riley, John
Riley, John Riley, my son. No, that was Lord Randall. Who
fain would lay, or lie, down. Got hold of a bad mussel. Or a cold
cockle. Something like that.

"Won't you come home John Riley, won't you come home,"
Tipton sang suddenly, loudly. "I cried the whole night
throoooo! Yee-AY!"

People looked at Tipton. He didn't mind. They always had,
even when he worked for Sears. Now, he had on shorts, a torn
T-shirt and moccasins. It was the way the beach people used
to dress in the drinking hour. He had seen no reason to
change.

He said to himself, "Full many a gem of purest ray serene,
the dark unfathomed caves of ocean bear. Yee-AY!"

Hey, that's all right, he thought admiringly. Goes with anything. Has a very ancient, wailing-wall quality. Very versatile.

They shall not pass. Yee-AY! On the beach of hesitation bleach the bones of countless millions who on the brink of victory paused to rest and waiting, died. Yee-AY!

"Yes sir, Mr. Tipton."

He was not drunk, he seldom was. He merely drank a lot.

The juke organ sang: "Under southern skies I walked with you, long ago when our love was new, in magnolia nights under scented skies but now the moon and I are blue, so blue, the moon and I are blue."

Cliff waited, but it was another song.

More people kept coming into the bar, to recuperate from a day of fresh air and sunshine. Most of them were tourists. Several recognized Tipton and whispered about it. He was seated on the end stool steadily eying the little gas bubbles going from left to right in the gaudy juke box. I haven't worked yet today, he thought, abstractly. But there is plenty of time.

"May I have your autograph, Mr. Tipton?" It was a stacked blonde burned bronze. Looking down her shirt front idly, he signed his name on a piece of paper. He never had figured out autograph wanters. She said thanks and undulated back to her table where love awaited, the assistant manager of a Katz drugstore in the Northland.

"See?" whispered Mrs. Rollero.

"Let's us," whispered Mrs. Holtman.

"Mr. Tipton?" a red-faced man said to Cliff.

"O.K., give me your pencil."

"What? Sure. Here." said John Riley.

Tipton signed his name on a bar napkin and handed it to John Riley and waited for the Yee-Ay song to come back. It did not occur to him to play it himself. For one thing, he didn't know how.

Riley stared blankly at the napkin with Cliff's name on it.

"Ha ha," Riley said tentatively.

Well, Tipton thought decisively, I'm not going to wait any longer. He was a sudden leaver. He walked rapidly from the bar toward his parked car, a three-year-old Ford. Riley waddled swiftly after him.

"Hey," Riley called. "I'm John Riley. I wanted to talk to you."

"Oh," said Cliff. "Sure. Well, hop in."

Riley grabbed Cliff's hand and shook it heartily. "Mighty glad to see you again, Cliff, old boy."

It was nearly a mile down the beach road to Tipton's home.

"I remember when this land along here was worth practically nothing," Riley said. "Shame we didn't buy it all up, eh, Cliff?"

"You want to go for a boat ride?"

"Uh. Why. Yes. Sure. I'd love it, Cliff."

Riley, on his short legs, trotted after Tipton who parked, walked in the back door of his home and, with Riley trotting at his heels, walked straight through the house, nodding to his wife and to a man asleep on the sofa. He went out the front door, down the beach to the pier, got into the boat the fathead publisher had sent him and reached under a seat for the screwdriver. With it, he punctured two cans of beer.

"Here," he said, handing one can to Riley and starting the engine.

Tipton's idea of a boat ride was to head toward the horizon as fast as he could go. For nearly an hour Riley sat petrified as the speedboat whipped toward Mexico like a crazed waterbug. Then with a sudden turn Cliff headed back toward Florida, moored and got out. Riley, soaking wet, clambered up on the pier and trotted after Tipton who went straight into his house, shook hands with Riley and said, "Well, I enjoyed it."

"Think nothing of it," Riley said confusedly.

Tipton went into the room where he worked, shutting the door behind him.

"Look out for the horse cars," said the man on the couch, in his sleep.

"He'll be in there for several hours," Trudy Tipton said. "Can I help you?"

"No, I guess not," Riley said numbly.

Dripping, he started the long walk back to the bar where his car was parked. *Now what the hell happened there?* he kept asking himself, walking wetly through the night.

Riley later made another appointment. Same place, same time. And he started off fine. He said, "Cliff, it's a dirty damn shame what's happening to Florida. At least to the coast of Florida."

However, he made the mistake somewhere in the conversation of mentioning his portable tape recorder—Riley dictated letters to himself as he drove—and Tipton immediately borrowed it to make transcripts of tourists talking.

The evening concluded with a Mr. Worthington, a liberal who operated a chain of car wash establishments in Memphis, Tennessee, doing imitations of a one-armed flute player, and no real estate was discussed. To Riley, Tipton became a challenge.

At one point John Riley was certain he had gotten his point across, at Tipton's home, when the author suddenly gulped his coffee and announced he had to go to Toronto, and did so. Some two weeks passed in this fashion and near the end of March Riley was in despair. He had heard that writers were impractical, but this was ridiculous.

If Cliff didn't break out on some tangent, somebody would come in and muddle his affairs. The Tipton home seemed a waystop for many unstable types, Riley felt. One night a literary agent who could recite a lewd version of "If" introduced a drink he called a Rammer, made of peculiar portions of anisette, vodka, rum and neutral grain spirits, and after four of these Riley fell to the floor and rolled under the sofa and Miss Murdine worried mildly about his whereabouts for two days.

At another point, Riley was introduced by Tipton as "My old friend, John Riley, who's in the insurance game."

If Riley hadn't been a real pro he would have given up. But he had a prospect and he had a potential deal. He knew he was wasting too much time on that particular matter, but it appealed to his sense of larceny. That he stayed red-eyed, nervous and jumpy merely spurred him on and for each delay he mentally added a hike in the price he was going to sell the Space place for when he bought it. That he woke up one morning in a motel outside Valdosta, Georgia, with no clear memory of how he got there, or why there was a land turtle in the bathtub wearing a placard which said, "Long Time, No Sea,"—all of this merely lent impetus to the chase.

He had decided to sell Tipton or perish.

"Have you been sick, John?" folks began to ask.

Mrs. Tipton, after all this, said to her husband, "Cliff, I wish you would quit torturing that fat little real estate man and go look at his house. It sounds good."

"I'm going to," Cliff said. "Quit nagging me."

Riley had as much will-power about drinking as the next red-faced Irishman. One night on a fishing boat that belonged to a friend of Cliff's, the writer looked down at Riley curled up in a coil of line on deck, holding a fourteen-pound red snapper to his chest.

"You say he sells storm windows?" Cliff's friend asked.

"He has the soul of a poet. Much stamina."

The sky was clear, the stars glittered, the boat swayed like a cradle and John Riley snuggled up with his fish and dreamed of that Great Development in the Sky.

He dreamed also of a docile Cliff Tipton signing papers. A pleasant dream it was, too, for John Riley who had persevered—who, since reading that first editorial, had pursued his prey, on through March and into April. Now it was April Tenth and Riley lay on deck dreaming his dream.

No hitches, nor obstacles were in his dream, nor was the fact the Yankee sister of Louise Antel had bought the Space place two days previously.

CHAPTER NINE

So WHEN WILL YOU LEAVE?" Art Rodes asked from his hospital bed. As coronaries go, his hadn't been a bad one. He would be back at work before too long.

"I'll work on through April and most of May," Paul said. "Then start packing and see about all the arrangements, and we'll leave as soon as Junior finishes the school term."

"You'll be happier," Art said. "I wouldn't. You will. Now here's one plot that will make you independently wealthy, alone."

Paul half listened to Rodes, waving his unlit cigar; spinning his never-ending preposterous ad-libbing. Paul stood there, staring out the hospital window at the lights, a big blunt man with a terrible sense of humor at what he had done. My God, he thought, I actually *quit*. He could hear the closing of all the frosted-glass doors, the soft but firm closing, the fencing out from the five-figure salaries.

I own a house in Florida, he thought, drawing hard on his cigarette, and I am going to make my living writing. My God.

Driving home from the hospital, he tried to place the fear which had been in his stomach ever since Betty had called and said she was buying the place. That had been ten days ago, and since she had been back home he had tried not to show the fear.

Suddenly, he remembered what it felt like. Once, years ago, on a southern paper, he remembered, he had been doing the safe-driving features for the holiday season. ("The message we want to get across," the publisher had explained, "is this: 'Alcohol and Gasoline does not mix.' What I want you should do is urge the fullest penalty of the legal machinery be imposed on them what get caught.")

Paul had written nine such stories and the night before Christmas got to drinking Southern Comfort with the printers and drove inadvertently into the statue of General Nathan Forrest in the center of the town square. He woke up Christmas morning in jail. He had jeopardized everything and his young wife was pregnant. And he had no excuses to give for himself, no matter how hard he pleaded there on the steel cot by the smelly toilet. Everything had worked out all right, no trouble. But it had been a time of intense fright and self-condemnation.

So is this one, he thought, turning into his driveway in Slathesdale—looking at his nice, secure home he would sell.

Of all the people he knew or thought he knew, Paul mused, only Otto Anvel—surprisingly—had accepted his explanation as to why he was leaving, and fully understood it; even more, in a way, than Art had.

He told Otto, simply, he was leaving a job he was unhappy in to try one he thought he might be happier in.

"I like you and I'll miss you," Otto had said, shaking hands, and emitting no mouthings about always-a-place-here-for-you. In his last weeks at Creation, Ltd., as the time for leaving neared,

Paul found his colleagues rather scornful beneath their façade of congratulations on "getting out of the old rat race," as they inevitably put it.

But also, as the weeks passed, Paul found the tight knot of fear untying within him. For the first time in a long time, as he went home early, and sober, from the office farewell party for him, he found himself looking forward, with the old anticipation, toward life.

He also found himself checking his bets, to the extent of thinking of his healthy bank balance and his blue chip stocks. The last night he got off the commuters' train he thought, Well, I can always come back.

"The hell you can," he replied, and strode the fourteen blocks home.

In late May the Vanningtons gave him a farewell party and all the quick people were there.

"So you're leaving the old rat race to really write," said the be-scarved author of one of the latest sex-in-suburbia volumes. The be-scarved author flung up his wrist sincerely. "To do something good and *lasting?*"

"Yeah," said Paul. "I got this dedicated feeling, like."

He and Betty sneaked away early. Nobody missed them. He was quite sure Slathesdale never would miss them. They went in to the city, to the top of a tall building. In the elevator he pinched her on the fanny. In the saloon on top of the building they drank a while. I own a house in Florida with no front door, he thought wonderingly, running his hands through his hair in sudden half-drunk delight, and I've never even *seen* the son of a bitch!

He could hardly wait to see it.

CHAPTER TEN

Paul—HIS LAST ROUND-TRIP TO
Creation over, the last hand-shakings done, the final bonus from
Otto received, the last firm closing of the frosted-glass door
executed—passed the first days of June being ordered about the
house by his wife and re-learning the fact he would never understand his children.

Lou was the one he had expected the protests from. The very
idea of breaking the news to her that she was to leave her
Slathesdale friends, the little theater and arty set, had appalled
him. To his astonishment, she turned out from the very first to
be thrilled by the entire idea.

"I think it's simply wonderful," she had squealed, when she
learned, for sure, he was quitting his job. "*Simply divine!* You're
an individualist! And at your age, too."

He had flinched.

Lou assumed a whole new role; she was a pioneer, braving
new horizons. She seemed disturbed they were to face the

frontier in a Pontiac station wagon rather than a covered wagon. Her eyes took on depth peculiar to those who have looked on distant and uncharted vistas.

She walked as if in buckskins. She did everything but roll her own. Her father was a free, unfettered artist, she told everybody. Her father (who was carefully working out his long-range stock dividend prospects) set his jaw each time he heard this, and flinched again.

Lou was going to be brave, brave all over the place. She seemed convinced the entire family faced economic disaster. She was noble. She said, "I don't have to go to any silly Eastern school. And you can cut my allowance."

"Oh, for Goodness sakes," her mother said. "We aren't exactly destitute, you know. After all."

But Lou, courageously, only put her arm around her feeble old mother's shoulders and patted her encouragingly, a girl pioneer in $18.95 slacks from Saks.

"No sacrifice is too much to offer to fight back at this age of conformity," she said. "I can work in the fields. They have lots of fields down there."

"Oh, make her shut up, Betty," Paul said, eying the rangy, shapely, near-woman who was his only daughter. A phase, he thought. She has been going through phases ever since she looked out through that maternity ward window. When the hell do they *stop* going through phases?

"We'll just all stick together," said Lou, little match girl in the snowstorm, lighting a cigarette in an ivory holder.

"Well," said Paul Higgins, Junior, whining, "I don't want to go to any stinking Florida with a bunch of stinking rubes and sit in a stinking tomato field the rest of my stinking life."

He seldom changed his adjective throughout all the last days of preparation for the move.

Paul had expected his son to be delighted at the prospect of change. Junior's tenth year had, up to then, been spent single-mindedly berating his environment: The cruddy kids in his stinking school, not to mention the Squaresville teachers; the stinking fact that there was nothing to do in the cruddy world around this feeby Slathesdale.

At the very mention of moving, however, he fell madly in love with his *status quo.*

"I'm sorry, Joe," he would whimper on the telephone. "I can't go to camp this summer. They're making me move away from all my friends. They don't care what *I* want. The stinking—"

"Make him cut out that stinking whining!" Paul bellowed, and left to talk with the lawyer who was handling the house sale and a few other loose ends. Well, Paul thought, driving to his attorney's office, I guess I'm glad that it's Lou who is for the move and Junior who is against it. I couldn't have stood it the other way around.

The week before school was out—bare days before the furniture was to be sent on ahead—Paul was standing by the kitchen sink pouring a shot of bourbon. Lou was outside in the drive talking to some of her friends.

". . . used to write excellent short stories," she was saying. "But the responsibility of a family forced him back onto the treadmill of conformity. Oh, Pamela, let's never burden *our* husbands!"

Paul choked on his bourbon.

Jamison (Cantaloupe-head) said firmly, "I will never marry until I have arrived fully, authorshipwise."

Spluttering, Paul spit his drink into the sink.

"Now that his children are nearly grown he's going back to the creative field," Lou said dramatically. "Junior, get away from here with those damn worms, *for the last time.*"

"Bunch of lily-livers!" Junior screamed happily.

"What's his book about?" Cantaloupe asked.

"He won't talk about it," Lou said soulfully. "A good writer never talks about the work in progress."

"That's not at all true. My dramatic coach is writing a novel and *he* talks about it. All the time. It's about this sensitive man who could have been a great actor but he wouldn't ever compromise his principles so, given his choice between becoming a great success or not compromising his principles he decides not to compromise his principles so he ends up a pitiably underpaid dramatic coach at a prep school where, ironically, he gets all the trappings of success after writing a book exposing prep schools and then—goddammit, Junior, get away with those worms!"

"Stinking sissy. Nasty worms, oo la la!"

Cantaloupe moved away from Junior and inquired, "What did your father do other than commercial stuff? I mean what did he ever do for the little magazines?"

Paul took his new drink with him, into the dining room where Betty was packing china in barrels.

"What did I ever do for the little magazines?"

"The what?" Betty said.

"The little magazines. The itsy-bitsy magazines?"

"Short short stories. Move that barrel over here."

Matter of fact, he thought, what *is* my book about? I better stick to short stories a while, he thought, until I see. My book doesn't expose anything, that's the trouble with it. Matter of fact, he thought, I can't think of anything to expose. No best seller there. Look at these "exurbia" boys they write about, he thought. Fully as glamorous as an air-conditioning convention. Not one in seven dozen is getting any extracurricular laying, whether through puritanical or physical reasons or plain lack of good old American know-how. Yet every little old novel they write has got to have passion in the garden and panting in the anteroom until you can't hear the creaky old prosaic truth.

Public relations is even duller than the newspaper business, he thought, but that kind of thing wouldn't sell. I don't have the right attitude, he decided.

He had read novels by folks in every trade from movie writing to commercial building and he was sick of them to the point of puking. They rose in a wailing chorus of I Was a Call Boy

for the Avenue, or Hollywood Made Me a Gilded Whore. Not
one of five hundred of those characters had any art to prostitute,
he thought, tossing back his drink, yet the fashion seems to be
to turn on whatever trade you get into and, with adolescently
braced teeth, try to rend the hand that fed or feeds you.

I simply don't get it, he thought. So who asked them? To
him, they sounded exactly like Junior whining, except they
didn't have the excuse of being only ten years old.

The fact was, he decided, it was simply lousy reporting by a
bunch of pseudo-literate Mickey Spillanes. At least Spillane was
honest about it—he indicated he was merely peddling what
the public wanted, and didn't play the social significance bit.
Angle, he amended, remembering James A. Wedley.

It's funny, Paul thought, that at age forty-five, I've got nothing
to expose. You can't tell people that. They would regard you
with suspicion.

I have covered police beats, city hall, every run. I did a series
on flagpole sitters. I have the inside dope on zoos. I have sat in
executive suites. Mine eyes have seen the glory of the coming
of MacArthur. In the asphalt wilds have I labored, in the toils
of commerce have I stooped.

Once I ran over Nathan Forrest. Sparkilite is an open book to
me; brake lining holds no secret nuance I cannot decipher.
Drunk have I been and sober, I have envied and been envied. I
have watched people very closely. They seem all right to me.
That will never sell.

Does this make me a dullard? No. But for the grace of
Providence I would have a two-toned dragon tattooed on my
chest from that time in Charleston. All the politicians I
ghosted speeches for got elected except that candidate in
Atlanta who got caught in the cathouse raid, and nobody could
blame that on me. I give to the poor, and would steal from the
rich given the opportunity. But what can I expose?

I know artists and writers and editors and executives and
reporters and drunks and conservatives and have been all these

things, and more, in various degrees. And yet never have I been able to discern that more than five per cent of the people in any field are out-and-out bastards, and maybe they have a reason. It seems unfair that ninety-five per cent of the books should be about that five per cent.

Fame is fickle and flitting brief, but once I was reprinted in Best Short Stories. I have been to the wars and back again and up on the tops of buildings. But, he thought, I will never be a "writer-type" writer, because everything seems too natural and I have no great protest to bitch about.

Anyhow, he thought, wrapping a pink saucer for the barrel, writer-type writers hurt too many people's feelings. They are going to "get it down on paper" if Mommy has the apoplexy all over Asheville; if hell freezes over, if divorces ensue and the rivers rise.

I, he thought, would rather make good cabinets. That being impossible I will then be a writer because that is all I know. What I want to do, he thought, is make enough money to live independently with my family and not have to do silly things I don't want to—not be nibbled to death by ducks, trampled by trivia.

You can polish a short story until it's pretty as a good cabinet and no good cabinetmaker is a hack.

My trouble, he thought, is that I won't compromise my lack of artistic integrity. He grinned to himself, a big-shouldered man, sitting cross-legged on the floor, wrapping china.

"Mr. Higgins?"

Paul looked up from his wrapped pink saucer.

A tall young man stood there, a friend of Lou's. He was going to be a writer. He had a salami sandwich in his hand, his left hand.

"Sir," he said to Paul, "I'm leaving tomorrow for a writers' conference. I may not see you again."

He grabbed Paul's hand and wrung it fervently. He said, "You have been a great inspiration to me."

He walked out, shoulders back, tripping over a boomerang on the floor.

Betty snickered.

Paul shrugged.

He was glad his wife was happy. He was surprised to find himself happy, happier than he had been in some time. And I can always come back, he kept saying, to the muffled thud of closing glass doors. I can always come back.

Junior slumped into the room, dejectedly holding his ice skates. Junior whined, "You can give these to some cruddy charity, I guess."

"Quit saying cruddy. Quit whining."

"I might as well throw all my stinking things away," Junior whimpered. "Nobody cares anyhow."

"Call me when you get to the boomerang."

CHAPTER ELEVEN

Despite the keening of Junior's whiner, it was a good trip south in the station wagon. The Higginses left in May, a few weeks after buying the house.

"Hey!" Paul said, a little before the Florida line. "I had forgotten about the moss."

"Stinking moss," said Junior from the back seat. Lou was asleep, legs sprawled, face innocent. Betty was making salami sandwiches to hold everybody until a late lunch. Paul drove an even sixty-five, staring in fascination at Florida.

It had been a long time since he had been in Florida. He had been a newspaperman on his last trip, some years back, on assignment to inquire into the reported revival of the Klan which had announced its intentions to discourage equality, by hanging folks to tall turpentine pines as the need arose. (The Grand Dragon had explained to Paul that this was part of a kick-off campaign to restore the fundamentals outlined by our forefathers.)

Paul was astounded at the growth of the state. He was eager
to see the house he owned. It was a long drive still, hundreds of
miles, and they had decided to stop somewhere in mid-afternoon
and rest for the night.

They stopped at a motel where the cottages were shaped
like cottages. Junior didn't like the stinking ocean. Lou found
a young man who took her for a walk on the pier. Betty Higgins
sat in the sand and hugged her knees and thought what a smart
wife she was. Paul Higgins looked at the surf and said, "That
place was making an old man out of me."

Louise Antel would have everything taken care of at the
new house. The furniture had been shipped in plenty of time.
Louise was the kind who took care of things. She always had.

She was sweeping the broad-screened porch when they drove
up the next day, the station wagon pulling and straining through
the sand road which led from the hardtop road down through
the live oaks, the pines, the citrus trees. An old birddog watched
them pass. He took long walks.

It was a light blue day, the breeze chased itself across the
peninsula, moving the trees in the sunshine. The air smelled
of faint wet and fresh greenness.

Louise Antel wore blue jeans. She was a thin, wiry, deeply
tanned woman with deep blue eyes and thick brows. She swept
with long, decisive strokes. The day before she had found a
ground rattler down by the lake and killed it with a hoe. The
day before that the moving men had come, a laconic driver with
a burly helper. They hated her in the morning, because she was
immediately boss, and loved her in the afternoon, because she
gave them red wine and spaghetti instead of the usual conde-
scending coffee.

Now, she stood on the porch looking at her only relatives.
The Higginses hadn't seen her yet. Junior climbed out, still whining. Poor pale little Yankee, she thought. Look at the feet on
that kid. He looks like a redbone hound pup.

Lou stood by the station wagon, dramatically inhaling the

pioneer-type air. That one will have the local stallions stomping, Louise thought. But she looks like she can take care of herself.

Betty Higgins was the first one to see Louise Antel and she ran across the yard to hug her sister.

Paul walked over. His sport shirt was unbuttoned all the way down, a red V of sunburn ran down his deep chest. He had on a long-billed Yankee cap. His gray-black hair needed cutting. A cigarette hung from the corner of his mouth.

"You've gotten fat, Paul."

He inhaled, and hugged his sister-in-law.

"Is this where we have to live?" Junior whined.

"Boy, how long has it been since you've had a really good switching?" Louise asked sternly.

He looked at his aunt, sizing her up. He made his decision, a wise one. He shut up like a clam.

A shriek of delight from the side yard. Lou called ecstatically, "Look at the lake. It's beautiful! I'm going in."

"It's all beautiful, Betty," Paul said. "Even more than you said."

Carefully, he crushed his cigarette with his heel. My land, he thought. He knew he was finally home. He walked into the trees, by himself. A certain breed of women know when to leave a man alone. He walked in that unconsciously baronial way all men walk on their own land. He picked up dirt and felt it.

None of the strangeness he had expected to be here was here. Until this very moment he had felt almost irresponsible over the entire move, to a wild place he had never seen; to a house with no front door.

But now he knew he was home. Here is where he would make his stand. He knew that, absolutely, as he walked in the solitude of the trees, near a moving river. New York was a memory already, neither unpleasant nor particularly pleasant. New York was neutral in his mind.

I saw the cities, Paul said, I did the distance.

Now I'll do some work.

The coffee was on the kitchen stove as he had known it would be, knowing Louise. The familiar furniture was in place. He saw the many things to be done, but there was no hurry.

That was the feeling he hadn't been able to place. That there was no hurry.

He and his wife and Louise sat at the kitchen table and drank black coffee and talked and there was no hurry.

Junior was happy with a terrapin he found.

After two days of pioneer life, Lou lost her pose and cried on her mother's shoulder, wailing for paradise lost and said she would shrivel and die for lack of what she termed intellectual companionship.

Paul set up his typewriter in an upstairs room where he could look at the lake and the woods. He kept expecting Indians to emerge and rather hoped they would. In the first week only one biped appeared, a rangy, tanned lad who was twelve and who shot a slingshot with the accuracy of a rifle.

Pale still, but no longer whining, Junior went into the woods with this little native and learned about slingshots and small game traps.

After a full week, Lou took to being withdrawn and wan and slump-shouldered—a rose born to blush unseen.

The drugstore in Flat City—it was a four-mile drive into Flat City—carried neither Theatre Arts, The New Yorker nor the Saturday Review.

But a young bronzed giant hulked on a soda fountain stool drinking something called a cherry phosphate. He wore army fatigue clothes and high-topped army shoes. A real clodhopper from way back, Lou told her mother—one with a vocabulary of about ten words.

But Lou went back to the drugstore, with a sidelong glance. And she had a cherry phosphate.

"What in the world do people do here?"

"Not much, I reckon. Pretty good show on tomorrow night in Fort Myers."

She told her mother she reckoned she would go with the clodhopper. It beat going insane. He could tell her all about plowing. So the next day the young man appeared.

Paul met the clodhopper and got his hand crushed in a handshake.

"How do, Mr. Higgins. I'm Tom Jedsoe."

Paul massaged his hand and looked thoughtfully at his daughter's date. From Lou's sarcastic description he had expected a real grits-mouthed bumpkin. This bumpkin was wearing an expensive sport coat and he drove a yellow Thunderbird.

Lou's jaw dropped when she saw the Thunderbird and Tom Jedsoe in his dress-up clothes.

"I'll take good care of your little girl," the bumpkin said, opening the car door for Lou; lighting her cigarette and sailing off in a cloud of sand. I'll just bet you will, Paul thought.

The next day Lou was not at all slump-shouldered. She was babbling. And then we went to the Coconut Room and then for a ride on his own boat and then and then and then . . .

"Who is this Tom Jedsoe?" Paul asked his sister-in-law, who was packing to go back to Guava Springs, having gotten her folks settled down. "For a farm boy he doesn't seem exactly destitute."

"Don't try to judge these people by how they act or look," Louise Antel told him.

As for Tom Jedsoe, she told Paul, he was a hard-working old cracker boy who got a GI loan, broke his own new ground with unpaid-for equipment, hit some good licks in produce and now owned his own fleet of refrigerator trucks plus a good portion of the northeast section of Flat County. And, Lou pointed out, because somebody doesn't talk much doesn't necessarily imply stupidity.

"Hm," said Paul, watching Jedsoe chasing his daughter into the lake.

Paul hadn't been able to figure out the people of Flat City insofar as their reaction to newcomers was concerned. He drove into town occasionally, to pick up something at a store—inevitably ended up at Flat City Pharmacy, the town's social center.

Everybody was very cordial but nobody expressed any curiosity about him. A stooped and seemingly vague little old man with bright blue eyes and a jawful of tobacco plumped down in a booth with Paul one day and introduced himself as Theodore J. Willingham, revealing that he put out the local paper, the weekly Ledger. Paul let the old man ramble on. The following week the drugstore clerk said, "What'll it be today, Mr. Higgins? Like this weather bettern Slathesdale?"

"How did you know I was from Slathesdale?"

"Why," the clerk said, "It was in the Ledger. Anyhow, we been expecting you folks since April."

Paul bought a copy of the local paper and looked at the item, on page three.

"The old Space place north of town has been purchased by Mr. and Mrs. Paul Higgins, formerly of Slathesdale, New York, who will make their year-round home here.

"Higgins was a vice president and account executive of the New York City public relations firm of Creation, Ltd., and prior to that was a newspaperman employed by several of the country's leading metropolitan dailies.

"He and Mrs. Higgins have two children, Paul Higgins, Jr., 10, and Miss Lou Higgins, 18. A recent visitor was Mrs. Higgins' sister, Mrs. Louise Antel, of Guava Springs.

"The Space place had stood vacant since the death of its builder, the late Ronald Space, in 1942. Higgins plans a complete renovation of the home.

"Higgins left the public relations field to devote all of his time to writing. He has had stories published in several major magazines."

Well, that tobacco chewing old galoot, Paul thought, admiringly. For the life of him he couldn't remember being pumped like that. He dropped the paper and walked over to the Ledger office.

Theodore J. Willingham was running off some job work on a Miehle vertical, and spitting on the floor.

"Like to subscribe to the paper," Paul said.

"Good. Four years or two?"

"Two."

"Good. I used to asked one year or two but everybody said one. It's better this way."

Theodore Willingham shoved the subscription money in his pocket and made a mark on the wall over the Linotype. He sat down at the Linotype and his fingers moved like a pianist's. The little shop was old and musty. The business office and the mechanical departments were in the same room. Willingham had one helper, a thin, bald, ancient man; a printer, who kept a jug of muscatel on the type case.

Willingham looked up pleasantly at Paul still standing there, staring at the hieroglyphics on the wall.

"Do all my bookkeeping on the wall," Willingham said. "You're supposed to ask me why."

"O.K. Why do you do all your bookkeeping on the wall?"

"Good. Because," Willingham said, "it saves paperwork."

The thin, wispy printer boomed off into frighteningly deep guffaws.

"Not a very good joke," Willingham said apologetically. "But he likes it."

Paul said, "About that story you did on me. That's the first time I've ever been on either end of an interview without knowing it."

Willingham nodded vaguely and kept playing the Linotype. He wrote directly on the machine, not from typed copy. Paul asked, "You've worked in other shops?"

"Here and there."

Paul pegged him as a tramp printer settled down. Willingham admitted to having worked in New York City. Where? On the New York Courier—it had been the most high-powered tabloid of them all.

"Ah," said Paul. "Linotype operator there?"

"Nope," said Willingham. "City editor."

A very strange town, Paul thought.

He said good-bye to Mr. Willingham. As he walked out, the editor called, "Paul."

"Yes?"

"Been looking forward to meeting you since we heard about the sale in April. Glad to have met you. You're going to like it here fine."

He would give himself a year, he could afford that. He would start by finishing one of the more likely half-finished short stories he had. He worked mostly at night on the story. In the daytime he fixed things around the house. He found the craftsmen around Flat City a peculiar bunch. They worked only when they damn well felt like it, but when a carpenter did carpentry it *was* carpentry. Not hack work. Betty was having some cabinets put in. The cabinetmaker bore the name of Funnelthroat Freely, due to his proclivity for alcohol. He made fine cabinets.

Paul finished his first story in a few nights, smoothed it, mailed it to his agent and started immediately on another.

Cosmopolitan magazine bought the story and asked for more.

Paul had forgotten the thrill of creating something, sanding it and selling it for money. He felt like a cub with his first byline, although he had been there before. He had, however, never sold a story before when his income depended on the stories' selling. He looked at his square hands and felt free. That was how he had wanted to feel and it was worth all the worry, worth it.

The story was about what happened to a man who had never had a sense of humor and was suddenly afflicted with one.

The night of the day the news came he went swimming in his lake with his wife, naked—here, in his own place he could do that for people left you the hell alone. He drank more than he intended to, celebrating. He got very egotistical and, sitting on the raft he had made of oil drums, sitting there in the black and starry night, he spoke of his potential artistry. Betty pushed him into the lake and he chased her through the woods.

"Let's go get dressed," she said, wrestling with him in the pine needles. "The kids will be back from the show. I don't think it would look right to Tom Jedsoe to see the potential grandparents of his children frolicking nude in the moonlight."

"Lord!" said Paul, suddenly sober. "Me. A grandfather."

"Well, not yet. But it does happen to people."

He walked toward his home which loomed in the dark. His wife looked interesting with no clothes on in moonlight, walking carefully around the sandspur patches.

"Well," Paul said, with a sudden thought. "I got out of that damn uniform, didn't I?"

She looked at him and laughed, "You sure did. And you're even losing your paunch.

He patted his naked, hairy, flattening belly happily.

When Lou and Tom and Junior returned from the movie, an hour later, Betty was knitting; Paul was drinking coffee and reading the local paper. Grand-paternally.

Junior was sent to bed, Lou and Tom went out and snuggled up in the front porch swing—they talked of middle age, and wondered how middle-aged folks stood the dullness of it all.

"Reckon you just get wore out when you're old," Tom ventured.

"I suppose." She asked if he had ever read Proust.

"Read it?" he said. "Hell, I can't even speak it."

She laughed girlishly and said, "Oh, Tom, you're so wonderfully primitive."

"Yeah," he said, pulling her close, moving in.

That morning on Guava Springs Key, Cliff Tipton had driven into his garage, stomped up on his porch and asked his wife, "*Now* what the hell are they building down the road?"

"A motel, Cliff."

"A motel? On the key road?"

"They don't have to be on highways any more. They can be anywhere. You know the name of this one?"

"Surf'n'Sex?"

"The Igloo."

"The *Igloo?*"

"The Igloo."

"*Igloo?*"

"Oh, stop! Yes, Igloo. You know that place outside Orlando where the units are shaped like wigwams? Well, as. I get it, these will be shaped like igloos."

"Well," said Tipton. "I've had enough. A goddamned nough. That rips it. That's the crop. Call John Riley. I'm ready to go look at that place down inland. Call him now."

"He'll be happy. He's been looking very bad."

Overhead, high over the Gulf beach, a blimp floated trailing a banner: "See Maniac Minsky for Used Cars."

A man came to the Tiptons' door selling a frozen food plan. The membership chairman of the Guava Springs Caribou Club came to the door to see if Tipton wanted to join. A carload of tourists pointed at Mr. Tipton. Down the road, the bulldozer grunted hungrily.

CHAPTER TWELVE

IN THE SHORT TIME SHE HAD lived in Flat County, now, Betty Higgins had developed her first real love for a place, for a piece of geography as such. It's what they mean by roots, she thought, working in the big kitchen, and the bromides are always true.

Junior was outside nailing the skin of an unfortunate small ex-mammal on a board. Lou was at the kitchen table taking off her Smouldering Flame nail polish because Tom had decided it was too loud. Aha, thought Betty, where now the bohemian blouses of yesteryear?

Upstairs the typewriter rattled, paused to think, clattered on.

Paul did not know how much he had changed and she had not told him yet, partly out of the Irish superstition that good things should not be mentioned or the witches will come and take them away. But he had changed, wonderfully. His mind was getting lean again. He drank for fun instead of anesthesia. Betty had known, much better than he, how unalive his routine at Creation had been making him. She would tell him how different he was now, but not until the time came—until the miracle was secure. He had always, back in New York, looked to her as though he were dressed up for a miscast role and the time he got a crew cut had made her sad.

And her son was no longer a poor pale little Yankee, as Louise had persisted in calling him, as if he were an escapee from a glass jar. It's funny, she thought, that despite being able to live in Slathesdale—or anywhere we wanted to up there—that there was really no outside in New York.

The typewriter was clattering steadily.

Thank you for that first story selling, she said to the saint in charge of such matters. Otherwise, he would have worried a little more, and talked and drank too much, and talked about how once you lose it you never get it back. I must have heard that a hundred times.

Her husband occasionally struck her as more than a little ridiculous, but he also occasionally impressed her. She felt this struck a nice balance. Some of his stories were very good. He had a strange, indirect way of saying something you didn't know was coming. His writing was entirely unlike him.

She went outside to go upstairs and the very act—having to go outside to go upstairs—put things suddenly in delightful focus for her, standing there in the clear day, by a house that swelled at the top. The solitude ancient as air.

I wonder, she thought, and laughed aloud, how the Books for the Poor drive is progressing?

Poor Alma Vannington, Betty thought in selfish delight, and poor the rest of them—piddling with plastic toothpicks and anxiously waiting for nothing.

"What's this, Mom?" Junior asked, ambling out of the woods, holding up a rusted object.

"A washboard."

"A what?"

"You wash clothes with it."

"It doesn't plug in anywhere."

"You just rub the dirty clothes on it."

"Is this what they used when you were young?"

"Yes. Before the invention of electricity. Now go play, I have to clean the upstairs."

Her days passed happily. She began to understand the strange holes in time. There always seemed to be plenty of time for things. There was no procession of men coming to the door— delivery men, salesmen, repairmen. She shopped in Flat City and it was as if she had lived there all her life.

She talked to people like Mrs. Jones who moved down from Racine thirteen years ago because of her husband's sinus. She talked to other people who said they seemed to get along better on less here than more in other places. These people were a tribe, a clan. Flat City was a little jog in time. It was nothing like the carnival of Florida, which Betty didn't like. One day in town she saw her husband across the street and for seconds did not recognize him. He walked slower, his clothing was baggy—and he looked quite happy as he ambled, looking slowly from side to side, to see.

He nodded easily to people in passing. Before, in the city, he had walked with long fast strides, his collar tight.

She loved these days, from morning to late night.

She cleaned the upstairs and walked down to the mailbox. There were three pieces of mail. Alma wrote to say she was keeping a close eye on the house, that a new couple, whose husband was a very witty writer for U.S. News & World Report, had moved onto the block, that Wilson Touhy had fallen off the wagon and gotten fired from Grinson & Wahlberg but fell into a much better job with Procter & Gamble and that other- wise everything was about the same although the "retreat" of the Higgins clan had certainly left a "hole" in everybody's social life. "Don't let the 'gators get you, darling. Ha, ha, ha."

The second letter was from Paul's agent who liked the plot of the last story he had sent but suggested it should be cut to a short-short.

The third letter was from Art Rodes and it said only: "Inasmuch as I am coming to visit you and stay a while, do you think that etiquette demands you invite me before or after I get there?"

The next day Paul wired Art: "Turn right at Jacksonville and ask at the filling station. You'll see our name on the mailbox. How is everything implementationwise?"

"What was that last word?" old man Wilson said at the telegraph office.

"It's foreignwise," Paul said, and spelled it out.

Outside, Flat City was nearly deserted. Old Man Willingham was sweeping out his shop with a long-handled push-broom. Mrs. Walling at Walling's Grocery sat asleep in the shade of a pine tree while Mr. Walling snapped pole beans.

The police chief, fire chief, magistrate and peace justice ambled down the street in the form of Chief J. S. Williams, a short fat man in blue overalls and a twenty-dollar Panama hat.

Chief Williams waved and Paul waved back.

Williams was a Flat City native, born and bred. He had only left Flat City once, to put in nine years in the merchant marine and go around the world several times.

Satisfied he was missing nothing, he came back home. He maintained his worldly manner. His collection of Panama hats was his pride. His black Mercury was his joy.

The first few years he had been police chief he had led a life of terrible frustration. He could catch no speeders. The ancient police car was easily outdistanced by everything else on the road. On dull nights the youth of Flat County found surcease from boredom by leading Chief Williams a constant and futile chase about the countryside.

Chief Williams pointed out it was a hell of a note when the chief of police couldn't even catch the local folk, much less the

Yankee tourists. The city fathers, for their part, pointed out there was no money for a new police car.

Williams put his mind to this problem. He asked and was granted permission to buy his own car and use city money for maintenance.

Consequently, once a year, Williams would drive into Miami, trade in his Mercury for a new one, buy several hats and return home. Now he felt equal. He fined speeders on a graduating level hinging on his own system which revolved around a combination of their politeness, where they came from and his snap decision of what the traffic would bear. If they were in a hurry he would hold court on the roadside.

He loved to park behind the big sign at the city limits which said, "WELCOME TO FLAT CITY" and doze, waiting for the very infrequent, and usually lost, tourist.

Also, the youth of Flat City respected Williams now, and drove quite safely.

The city coffers prospered.

Chief Williams also made a fine fire chief, it was agreed, far superior to his predecessor who had garnered local fame by neglecting to keep gas in the old La France fire engine. The fire engine, loaded with volunteers, had run out of gas twice en route to fires.

A bucket brigade had saved the lumber yard, but the Bright Light Lounge on the edge of town had burned to the ground while the former chief sat on Main street whirring the starter of his fuel-less chariot and cursing.

Paul drove down Main Street, liking his adopted town. Jack Haney and his cronies sat playing their never-ending game of pinochle in the old, cool-smelling and tile-floored Flat City Sundries, catty-cornered from the drugstore.

Haney sold thread, ribbon, yard goods, etc. He was a successful business man.

He hadn't meant to be. He had just wanted to play pinochle in the Flat City Sundries in his declining years after a life spent God knows where and doing God knows what.

But a chain store bought out Flat City Sundries and the new manager, in rimless glasses, said, "I can't have you old men cluttering up the place with card games all day and night."

"Is that so?" said Jack Haney, and went to his room and got out his silk business suit that had hung undisturbed for several years.

"Where are you going?" sniffed his old-maid sister, who taught geography and to whom Jack was a cross, burden and a ne'er-do-well.

"Out," Haney said, lifting one corner of the rug in his small, bare room and getting his folding money.

He stayed gone for nearly ten months and when he came back he walked into Flat City Sundries, wearing a new silk suit just like the old one, and showed the manager some papers proving he owned the place and he said, "You're fired. Get your tail out of here."

He put away his silk suit and never put it on again. He hired a young man to run the Flat City Sundries and Jack Haney and his cronies played pinochle there day and night. His sister was proud of him because he was a successful merchant.

Paul waved at Haney, who waved back.

I wonder, Paul thought, grinning, what Art will think of this town? Art will get the pitch, he thought. Art always does. It may take him a few days.

Paul turned into the Standard Oil.

A big black car with a New Jersey tag was parked under the overhang.

"Fill her up, boy," the tourist said to the filling station proprietor. "Check the water and tires. I don't suppose you have any good cigars?"

"There's a box of Hav-a-Tampas on the counter in yonder," said Jason Twig, the proprietor.

The driver, wearing shorts, a duckbilled cap, his stomach protruding under his yellow sport shirt, cast his eyes to heaven.

His wife, an irritated skinny woman in orange slacks and Roman sandals which caused her to lurch about in all directions, said, "I have to go. You suppose it's decent?"

"So go already," snapped her lord and protector. "How would I know?"

"You want the ethyl or the regular?" asked Jason Twig. "The regular is the cheap."

"Ethyl, of course," the tourist snarled. "Is there a decent restaurant anywhere on this godforsaken road?"

Paul was content to sit and watch. Jason had a good act.

"Lessee now," Jason said, after a maddeningly long time. "A restaurant."

"Oh, God," snarled the tourist. "Never mind. Hurry up. Which is the best way to Fort Lauderdale?"

Jason studied this at length and finally said, "What you do is you go back that way you come about sixty, sixty-five miles and turn left."

"I knew it, I *knew* it!" The tourist was hitting himself in the head with his clenched fist. His wife lurched back. He spoke rudely to her, saying her aunt in Fort Myers should go to a head doctor, her and her short-cuts.

"If you can wait around til about five, five-thirty," Jason said, "The PTA is fixin' to have a fishfry down at the school."

Jason watched the tourist car roar away.

"Figure Chief Williams will get about fifteen, eighteen bucks out of that one," he said to Paul. "Haste makes waste. How goes it, Paul?"

"Fine, Jason. Ten regular. And you?"

"Fine. Got a letter from my boy in the navy. He got through flying school, proud as a little old eagle. Sent a picture. Most conceited expression I've ever seen, in that uniform. Think I'll sic him on that daughter of yours."

"Better warn him Tom Jedsoe is an ex-platoon sergeant, or your flyboy might get grounded in a tomato patch."

"Hear you sold another story. What about?"

"It's about a C.P.A. who wanted to be a croupier."

"He make it?"

"Sort of."

Jason nodded. "They say everything is autobiographical. How you liking it here?"

"I like it here."

"Pop," said Junior, when Paul got home, "are we ever going back to New York?"

"I don't think so."

"Good. I'm learning animal stuffing."

"You smell like it."

From his upstairs workroom, he could not see the river for the trees but he knew it was there. He could see one edge of the huge lake. He reread the first sentence of the story he was trying to cut.

"No man is a conformist, not really," he read. "He may want to be one, may try like hell to be one—but around the corner of time stands circumstance, awaiting us all."

"Crap," said Paul, and penciled the paragraph out. "You're supposed to get right into it. You know that as well as I do."

For supper they had snap beans, pot roast, biscuits, mashed potatoes, slices of tomatoes big as softballs and red as remembered Octobers. He worked late, and near midnight heard somebody pounding on the front wall.

He went downstairs and hollered, "There's no front door. Come around."

A big, bearlike man followed by a short fat man came around to the side.

"No front door," the big man said. "Hell of a good idea. I'm Cliff Tipton."

"You are?" said Paul, shaking hands. "I'm Paul Higgins. I've been reading your stuff since the old Street and Smith days."

"No kidding," said Tipton. "This is John Riley."

"What're you drinking?"

"Orange gin," said Tipton.

"I don't have any," Paul said. "Can offer you—"

"I've got some," Tipton said. "Get it, John."

Riley and Tipton had left Guava Springs Key before dark. Tipton had called Riley and said, "I'm ready, John. Come help me make the deal and get your commission."

Tipton drove south down the Tamiami trail at an even fifty, autos whipping past him seeking Florida. When he turned left across the state, long after dark, he slowed even more. The flatlands spread under the moon like a dark blue blanket, glinting wetly in the moonlight nuzzling the blue-black lakes. At a rickety bridge frogs sounded a deep chorus and Tipton stopped and listened and said, "aha, aha," and nodded his head approvingly. He got out to listen. Riley rummaged through the glove compartment and came up with a bottle. "Orange gin?" Riley said. "This glove compartment of yours is ruining my stomach." Riley took a deep swig.

It was nearly midnight when they came into Flat City. Cliff looked at the firehouse, the drugstore, the hardware store, the filling stations, the bank, the single two-story office building, the courthouse. Nobody was on the street.

Cliff nodded again to himself. One light was on, in the Flat City Ledger and a job press was clanking.

"Miehle vertical," Riley said. "Sometimes I miss the newspaper business."

"All poets are nostalgic for what never was."

"Hell, I couldn't even make my car payments."

Riley watched carefully for the road. It was the third time in his life he had ever been in Flat County. The last time had been in the middle of March, to drive down to make sure the house was in something approaching passable condition, so he could buy and sell it.

They found the road, on the third try. They drove down the sandy moonlit ruts. A station wagon was parked at the Space

place and a light was on upstairs. *What the hell?* Riley thought
in sudden alarm. There was nobody here a few weeks ago.

"This is what I want," said Tipton. "This stockade."

"Er," said John Riley. "Somebody seems to have—ah, that
is, somebody apparently—"

"John," said Cliff, "Don't worry. Don't worry—we'll just buy
it from these folks. You've earned a commission."

"You *knew* the place wasn't, exactly, so to speak, in my immediate possession?" He was a real estate man.

"I used to be assistant credit manager for Sears," Cliff said,
on the porch. "Where the hell's the door?"

He was pounding on the wall when somebody called to come
around to the side.

"Not for sale." Paul Higgins grinned, after they were all seated
in the kitchen, drinking.

"Name your price," Cliff said. "Don't skimp. I'm up to my
knees in money now."

"Now Cliff," said John Riley, alarmed. "As your adviser I—"

"Not for sale," Paul said. "Not after what I've been through.
I like it here. Here I stay. How come you want it?"

"Same reason you do, I think," Cliff said, looking closely at
Paul Higgins. "Yes."

"Hey!" Riley said, looking at the open door of one of the
new cabinets. "Is that a case of Mount Vernon Rye?"

"Indeed," said Paul. "Water or soda?"

Cliff and Paul talked a long time. It is always surprising to
meet a friend. It makes you wonder how many you pass on the
street, forever unmet, and that makes you sad.

About three o'clock they tucked Riley into slumber by the
stove on the dog's blanket after he insisted he preferred it to the
sofa. (Junior had acquired the dog, a rangy hound adolescent, in
trade for a dollar and his ice skates.) "Room service?" Riley
mumbled. "Call me at eight. Big deal tomorrow." The dog
glared at him.

"Won't sell the place. Well, all right," Cliff said.

"It's not that I'm not practical. I am."

"Me too. You want to hear my theory?"

"No, I want to tell mine."

"We'll flip. Loser has to fix the drinks and go last."

"Good. Got a coin?" Paul asked.

"No."

"Well, you go first."

"No, you."

But they had both forgotten their theories.

CHAPTER THIRTEEN

*"News is one of the most important things
in a newspaper, by and large."*
From an address by Harrington
Space to the Guava Springs
Advertising Club

Other than for some wor-
risome tribulations caused by his son, Jerry, who was learning
the creative end of the business, the spring and early summer
had been a fine period for Harrington Space.

Ad lineage was up in most of his newspapers, and so was
circulation. The sole exception had been the Papaya Beach
Gazette where the trouble had been traced to the editor. He
had been spending most of his time writing the definitive
explanation of the value of a free and informed press, it was
learned, and sending back public domain boilerplate, such as
Emerson's essays, to be set in type for the paper, rather than

concentrating on local news. Now he had been discharged, however, and replaced by a sound young man who thought of Emerson in terms of electrical appliances and also was willing to work for $18.50 a week less. So, even this small link in the Space chain had not only been repaired but strengthened.

Harrington Space, by and large, had tasted life during this period and found it good.

The Sunshine State continued to boom and the Shiny Bulldozer was on the march. Mrs. Space had taken to good works at the national level and stayed out of town with commendable frequency; Harrington's digestion was better than it had been in years.

The weather ball was already atop Progress Tower and the dedication was now only bare weeks away. Harrington could hardly wait to move in. In his new building he would have a private elevator and a public address system which, by dint of pushing little buttons, could reach any given room in the tower, or, by pushing all the buttons, *everyplace* in Progress Tower. "Team," he would be able to say, "this is the chief."

The thought reminded him he hadn't written an A.P.B. (all points bulletin) memo for several days. So he wrote one.

"Memo all editors. Concentrate on delinquency. Watch for upcoming signed editorial. Want tear sheets what being done about delinquency. Remember, delinquency begins at home."

Reading it over he chanced to think of Jerry and marked out the last sentence. Then he gave the memo to his secretary who rushed to Duplicating with it.

Harrington walked to the window of his office and looked out over Guava Springs. He stood there with his hands folded over his shirt front, his round red face solemn, his lips pursed in thought. He rocked back and forth on his heels, concentrating. A blimp went by. It trailed a banner. "MANIAC MINSKY FOR USED CARS."

"Hm," he said disapprovingly. Newspapers are the best proven ad medium, dollar for dollar. Not blimps.

Guava Springs was growing with remarkable rapidity, he thought with pleasure. Another big motel was going up east of town and still another out on the key. The one east of town would have cottages shaped like little ante-bellum mansions, and a split-level swimming pool. Theater-in-the-round had been put in the old public square. The city park, which had nothing but trees and shrubbery in it anyhow, was being paved for a fine parking lot, with places for hibiscus bushes right in the asphalt. More writers and artists kept moving in over on Guava Key. Tipton kept winning prizes. He was really putting the key on the map.

More and more culture was coming in. On Saturdays when it was hard to fill up the paper without paying overtime, Harrington often had culture stories about the writers and artists. With such interviews, and the church news which was kept in type, that pretty well took care of the inside of the second section.

He wrote another memo: "Be sure line up Tipton for dedication ceremony." He had called Tipton, but Tipton's butler had said he was on an extended caribou hunting expedition. Writers lead interesting lives, Space thought. But are poor credit risks.

He glanced at his watch. Jerry was thirty minutes late. Harrington sighed.

That boy has got the stuff, basically, he thought. It's merely a question of finding the right outlet. It would help, he thought rather irritably, if he would keep his hands out of the damn machinery. And off of women.

Jerry's latest assignment, down on the east coast, hadn't worked out at all well. He had been assigned to look into the Florida hotel industry and narrowly escaped a charge of attempted bribery of a house detective.

Jerry had denied all, saying there was no such thing as *attempted* bribery of a house detective, but nevertheless it had cost money to shut the thing up. How would a thing like that look in the newspapers?

Harrington thought briefly of having Jerry head up the delinquency series, but immediately thought better of it.

What that boy needs is a challenge. I know he's got the stuff. Space nodded decisively.

"Whoooop!" shrieked Harrington's secretary in the outer office. "You son of a—oh. Hello, Mr. Space."

Jerry Space had arrived. He strode in, tall, thin, a cigarette in a long holder, wearing a plaid Ivy league cap on his crew cut.

"What's the word, Daddy-o?" he said. "Sorry I'm late. My calendar didn't go off."

Harrington drummed studiously on the desk with his finger tips. Jerry put his feet on the desk and lighted a new cigarette from the old one.

Harrington looked up suddenly. "Son— I know you've got the stuff."

Jerry's eyes veiled, became wary.

"What stuff?"

"Ability. Potential."

"Oh," said Jerry, relieved. "That."

"It's just a question of finding the right channel."

"Well, don't send me on any more cattle stories."

"No, no. You need a real challenge."

"You think trying to outrun that bull wasn't a challenge?"

Jerry had chosen to start research on his cattle industry in a wooded area near Kissimmee with the cooperative daughter of a cattle rancher, but his research had been interrupted by the arrival of a prize bull. The girl, cattle wise, merely jumped up and stood behind a tree but Jerry, in a state of disarray, made the mistake of trying to outrun the bull on the straightaway. It ended in a tie with Jerry atop a barbed wire fence where he had been boosted by the bull. The girl got so tickled he never finished his research.

"Someday, son, you will take a responsible position at the tiller of this organization. You will have to take the bull by the horns."

Jerry winced.

"You will have to put your shoulder to the wheel and your nose to the grindstone."

"Simultaneously? While keeping a stiff upper lip and never saying die?"

"Right!"

"What an appallingly awkward position. Would I be carrying a big stick while walking softly, or keeping my powder dry?"

His father ignored him. He said, "I think perhaps the trouble has been trying to put a race horse into a plowhorse's job. You needed to explore, learn. You need to learn *the concept end of the business!*"

Jerry watched the secretary sidle in, sidle out.

"Yessir!" Harrington said. "Think big!"

"I am, I am." Jerry watched the secretary's departure.

"Now what are we trying to do here?"

"Make more money."

"Well, ah, yes. The prime function of a publishing business is to exist. However—the concept is something else again. Son, you are going to learn Florida like it has never been learned before!"

"Huh?"

Harrington began to pace, as tycoons do in the movies. "Here is the greatest story on earth—the Sunshine State! You are going to *saturate* yourself in its history. You are going to become *the* authority on Florida! You will visit the factories, the hamlets, the shores. You will talk to leathery farmers in fertile fields. You will talk to bulldozer operators. To the rich, to the poor— what poor we have—and to the Everyman, whose name is legion."

"John Q. Doe?"

"Right! You will set out and learn this state like it has never been learned before. You, son, will grasp the concept of Florida!"

"What will I do with it?"

"Your series," said Harrington impressively, "will be carried on the front page of every Space paper—perhaps published in book form. It will be the making of you."

"Hoo," said Jerry, impressed despite himself. "That's a big order. That could be work."

"You will consider yourself a scout in a pioneer nation," Harrington said, rising, putting his hand on his son's shoulder. "Consider the valuable background we of the Space team will have as the result of your down-to-earth explorations in concept."

"Do I get a raise?"

"We can talk about that later," Harrington said instinctively. "Anyhow, son, here is a challenge. Go . . . and do a bang-up job. I know you will. Because, down under, you have the stuff. *Consider yourself Florida's biographer!*"

Shoulders back, Jerry strode from the office.

"Gimme a pad of expense vouchers," he said to the secretary. "And what are you doing tonight?"

"A reporter asked me today what I was thinkin'," Joe Steblunk told his wife at the supper table.

"What you was thinking?"

"Yeh. While I was pushin' the dozer around."

"So you said?"

"I said it seemed a shame to knock the trees down."

"What did he say?"

"He wrote it down."

Florida ranks as the twenty-first state of the union in area, the twenty-seventh in order of admission to the Union. Except for the region contiguous to Alabama and Georgia, Florida comprises a peninsula of the North American Continent, projecting southward between the Atlantic Ocean and the Gulf of Mexico for a distance of about 375 miles. The width of the peninsula averages about one hundred miles. The coastline is longer than that of any other state of the union.

The flora and fauna of Florida are widely diversified, with species common to both temperate and semitropical regions. The first European known to have visited the southeast peninsula of the North American mainland was the Spanish navigator, Juan Ponce de Leon, in March, 1513.

He led an expedition westward in search of an island which, according to native lore, was the site of a fountain of youth.

He cruised along both coasts but failed to locate it.

During the next forty years Florida was visited by additional explorers but continuing native hostility discouraged attempts at colonization.

CHAPTER FOURTEEN

TWELVE THOUSAND CARIBOU TO March Down Biscayne Boulevard."

"What?" said Arthur Rodes to himself. "What?"

He read the story under the headline in the paper in his Miami hotel room.

"Hilarity and hi-jinks tonight will mark the official opening of the ninth annual convention of the Benevolent and Fraternal Order of Caribou."

"Oh," Art said. "Oh."

"More than twelve thousand conventioneers were expected to have registered before kickoff time of the gala opening parade at 8:30 p.m.

"Osgood R. Rutherford, an umbrella manufacturer of Tucson, Arizona, outgoing president of the organization, stressed that a serious goal underlies the fraternal aspects of the convention.

" 'We are sailing ahead under full canvas toward reaching our campaign goal of complete construction of Caribou Care Center,' Rutherford asserted."

If there is anything I can't stand, Art thought, tossing the paper aside and lying back on the hotel room bed, it's an assertive caribou.

He reached for the phone, placed a call to Mr. Paul Higgins of Flat City. He looked out the window over the bay. Boats skeetered. He chewed on his thin cigar, unlit. Except for Dubonnet and a little sherry he hadn't drunk much, either, since his coronary in February. Now it was July. They said he was good as new. Practically.

Art had come in by plane, grabbed a cab. He planned to spend a few weeks in Florida. Part business, mostly vacation. The business part took care of expense accounts. Otto was good about that. Art was looking forward to seeing Paul, Betty, the kids. ("Take a good rest," Otto had said. "Also, see if he's ready to come back yet.")

Art had arrived the previous day. He talked to a brake-lining baron. He took the baron's niece to dinner. Art had a beautifully grained wallet. It had many credit cards in it.

"Unkie thinks you're the most," the niece had said.

The music had been low. A sub-waiter brought a fresh bowl of poinciana blossoms in a ceramic bowl filled with round ice cubes. Art had sipped his Dubonnet, eyed the niece's cleavage and taken the sheaf of cards from his wallet.

The cigar in his teeth tilted up at an angle and he dealt the credit cards off, one by one. The pasteboards fell, slap, slap, and somewhere a paddlewheel churned. Art produced the right card and signed, put the deck back in his derringer pocket. He was a good public relations man.

"Have you seen Biscayne Bay by moonlight, dear?"

"It's raining." she said, sadly.

"I didn't mean go outside."

It had been a fine evening and his room had an excellent view. This morning he had planned to take a train into Flat City. But the station man said that was impossible.

"Why?"

"No tracks," the man said. "That's why."

So he had called Paul.

"I'm at the Surfspray Spa in a place called Miami Beach," Art said to Paul. "What do I do now? Swing in on a vine?"

"I'll drive over and get you."

"Oh, hell no."

"Sure. A friend of mine here visiting has been wanting to visit Miami and I've never been there. We'll leave after lunch, and pick you up around six or seven. Wait in your room."

"What friend? Do I know him?"

"Cliff Tipton."

"What's he doing there?"

"You should have seen the real estate man we had under the stove. Anyhow, we'll see you. Good to hear you."

"Good to hear you."

Art hung up and looked out the window. Three convention delegates from Little Rock went out on the beach in funny hats. A barefoot tycoon with cheek of tan touched a calloused toe in the hotel pool and hitched at his baggy trunks. "What's a lox?" said a plumber from Houston. Breeze Zephyr, interpretive dancer who twirled tassels with her torso, slept in a poolside chair and dreamed she was back milking on the farm in Wisconsin and did not know if it was a good dream or bad.

One hundred and forty-five press agents were going out for coffee or a drink. Five Caribou started a crap game in 911. The day was passing. The Chamber of Commerce was active. A light haze was on the bay.

Miami under the late afternoon sun waited for the night. All the neon was ready. The strippers awakened and looked in the mirrors at their eyes. The good girls sat at their typewriters, waiting for five o'clock and wondering if tonight would be the night—saying, we'll see, we'll see.

The automobiles raced in from the North, sleek as sweaty otters, honking like ulcerous geese.

Originally there were six Miami tribes, including the Pia and the Wienkensaw, and the few remaining survivors live in Indiana and Ohio.

"Low down payments!" said the signs with fluttering banners, gay as pirate sloops. A breeze comes off the bay and the Chamber of Commerce remains active. A tired old real estate promoter who has made, and lost, three fortunes sits in the park and stares at his runover shoes, wonders if he should make another fortune—decides he might as well, there's nothing else to do. A cobbler sticking to his last.

Five o'clock and Art Rodes went to the rooftop saloon to the Unicorn Room. A unicorn is an animal with one horn which doesn't exist, if you put the wrong construction on it, Art thought.

A drinker chortled to his companion, "So I said what's the matter with you, you anti-bigot?"

"Oh you silly," said the sheathed girl.

This was the nation's playground.

At the long bar sat a loner; introspective, drunk. He nodded to Art and said, "Sir, we are lost and sinking."

"The glory that was Greece," said Art. "The grandeur that was Rome."

"I'm from Cleveland."

"I'm not," Art said.

"That's something."

Far out in the workaday world the quitting-time traffic was moving. The loner looked into his glass and smiled a secret smile. Art sipped his sherry and watched the people. He was a people watcher. A captain of industry strode in trailed by lackeys and Art watched him with a professionally piratical eye. The magnate sat and spoke of his sinus, loudly for all to hear. It was better, except for this dull pain right here.

The loner said, "Better one glimpse in the tavern caught than in the temple lost outright."

"Where now the snows of yesteryear, whence gone the whooping crane?" Art replied.

"You're all heart, my friend. I like you. How does one get to Cleveland from here?"

"Straight up and scatter out."

"Never give your right name, old buddy."

"Cheers."

It was getting darker in the nation's playground. Art went back to his room, to wait. Miami, he thought. What a peculiar place. The small amount of very good sherry had lulled him. He went to sleep.

Paul and Cliff left in plenty of time to get there. Plenty of time to get there by six, seven at the latest.

"Look at that," Cliff kept saying, watching the carnival of Florida's lower east coast go by. "My God, Paul, look at that!"

Cliff had borrowed one of Paul's suits. He had to wear the coat because the pants wouldn't button. He looked quite Ivy League, except for being barefoot.

Paul was driving the station wagon. John Riley had taken Cliff's car back to Guava Springs two days ago, along with two fifths of Mount Vernon rye.

A house trailer made of aluminum came by.

"When I moved out on my key," said Cliff, "You could walk miles down the beach. By yourself and nobody. Now it's getting like this."

"That's a damn shame."

They stopped for a drink, was what threw them late.

Buttoned-up, Tipton in his, or rather Paul's, suit, looked like a successful advertising man.

Paul wore a sport shirt. So the bartender in the Chez Chum Lounge where they stopped deferred to the dressed-up Tipton.

"Yes *sir!*" said the sleek bartender, who wore a red cummerbund and looked like a successful weasel.

Cliff ordered two Singapore slings made of scotch. The bartender didn't change expression. The waitress did. She was the only one who had noticed Cliff was barefooted. Seated at the bar, he was scratching the sole of one bare foot with the big toe of the other.

They drank and talked a while.

"CARIBOU COMBINE BUSINESS, PLEASURE!" said the headline on a paper on the bar.

"I should have become a Caribou," Tipton said, snapping his fingers. "They asked me."

"Yessir," said the bartender.

"Are you a Caribou?" Cliff asked Paul, who hadn't noticed the paper. Paul looked at him.

They stopped at a couple more bars. Then they ran into the afternoon traffic in outlying Miami. They stopped at a bar to wait out the traffic. Cliff ordered rye martinis. Several members of the Philadelphia chapter of Caribou were in the bar preparing for the parade. Paul and Cliff learned the Caribou yell.

> Caribou, caribou, caribou all
> Caribou, caribou, sound your call
> AH'WHOOOOOOOOOOOOOO-WAH!
> Caribou! Caribou! Caribou all! ONE FOR ALL!"

Then they sang you tell me your dream and I will tell you mine.

Then Cliff and Paul, who had let time slip by, ran into the traffic of the Caribou parade. Cliff felt he should march in it. Paul said he really didn't feel qualified. Cliff swore him in. They parked in a small park with a statue of Diana, goddess of the hunt, and joined the Birmingham chapter as it came by.

Paul decided he was beginning to feel his drinks. Well, he thought, I haven't been out at night for some time.

The Birmingham chapter tootled bagpipes. The Rapid City boys were counting cadence. The lads from Memphis led a goat. The Detroit contingent rode a Model-T Ford that bucked up on its hind wheels. The moon was three-quarters full.

"Caribou, Caribou, Caribou all!" Cliff was shouting.

"What I like about Flat County," shouted Paul, rather

thickly. "Is you can always drive into the city and catch a play!" He was marching erect, stiffly, carefully.

"Look, Mommy," said a little boy with a balloon. "That one doesn't have any shoes on."

"Let's get in with the bagpipes," Paul said.

The parade weaved along. All the lights were pretty. Then, Paul noted, there was one big pretty light, like a rainbow. Shoulders back, he walked toward it and passed out in a used car lot.

When the parade had gone, Cliff hailed a cab and took him back to the station wagon. Then Cliff took a little nap. It was well after midnight when he awakened.

"Let's see," Cliff said to himself. "That was the Surfspray Spa? Yes. Correct."

He drove to Art's hotel. Paul was snoring in the back seat. Cliff borrowed his shoes.

The lobby of the Surfspray Spa was thick with Caribou and with delegates to the convention of the DeJays Advisory Council.

Was that room number 909 or 919? Cliff wondered. He decided it was 909. He asked the clerk for the key and got it. He stopped by the Polka-Dot Room for a drink before going up after Paul's friend. He pulled a wad of currency from his pocket, crumpled as he always carried it. The platinum blonde on the second stool clicked her eyes toward it.

"Give me six or eight martinis in a bottle," Cliff said to the bartender. He felt he should take Paul's friend a drink. The bartender, bowing and scraping, and eying the currency, said he just happened to know where he could get a bottle of ready-mixed martinis.

"Fine," said Cliff. "Give me one while I'm waiting. Give her one, too."

"I don't usually drink with strangers," she said coolly. "However."

"What is a girl like you doing in a place like this?" Cliff asked. He explained he owned a chain of egg factories and was very rich. He had decided it would be a nice gesture to take her to Paul's friend, with the drinks. Because it would make up for being so late.

"Take this on account," he said, slipping a bill into her palm. He had the instincts of a bellhop. "And come up to 909 in a few minutes."

"Got you," she said. He ambled off with the bottle of martinis, his Caribou hat square on his head. He had borrowed it from a prone Philadelphian. He went up to 909. He unlocked the door. Inside, somebody was snoring and—at that instant— he heard a loud voice from 911 next door inquire, "Who'll fade me? Shooting the bundle."

"Nine's the point," came the reply.

"Well," thought Cliff happily, reclosing the door of 909; leaving the key in the lock. "My favorite sport."

He knocked on the door of 911. The group of Caribou shooting craps welcomed their unknown brother. Cliff got the dice and made four straight passes before he lost the dice. "A fine game," he said. "I will give Art a buzz, awaken him and have him scoot over."

Still on his knees he reached up for the phone and told the operator. "Give me Art Rodes' room—909."

"There must be some mistake, sir," the operator said. "Suite 909-907 is occupied by Mr. Osgood Rutherford, president of the Caribou. I will get your correct room number. Rodes? That is 919, sir, and I am ringing."

"Ullo," came Art's sleepy voice.

The blonde's expression was regal. No expression is so regal as that of a free-lance call girl in a Miami Beach elevator, en route to her job. She walked, with swaying hips, down the ninth floor corridor. She turned the key she found in the door of 909. A sliver of light from the bathroom barely showed the outline of the furniture. She put her purse by the three-cornered hat.

"I'm here, hon," she said to the form supine in the bed,

pulling her dress over her head. "Did I make you wait?" She unsnapped her bra, stepped out of her pants, sat on the edge of the bed. Osgood Rutherford, tired from the evening's honors as outgoing president, sleeping soundly in righteousness, dreamed of steady rainfall and upgoing profits of his umbrella manufacturing concern. "Where'd you put the liquor, sug?" the naked young lady inquired, bending over and biting him on the ear. "Ooga!" went Mr. Rutherford, sitting bolt upright in bed.

At that precise instant the room was flooded with light and Mrs. Osgood Rutherford, who had been kept late at the Ladies' Auxiliary campaign dinner, stood corseted and blinking in the doorway.

Art Rodes, wishing for a cigar, came sleepily out of 919, turned toward 911 to accept Mr. Tipton's invitation.

A young lady sallied forth at top speed from 909, stuffing undies in her purse and trying to pull her dress below navel level. A wild-eyed man in purple pajamas followed, making incoherent noises and traveling fast. Right behind him in pursuit was a moutainous lady wearing a badge which said "Willing Worker" and screaming imprecations; meanwhile flailing at the gentleman with a malacca-cane umbrella, Heavy Duty Model 103A.

This procession swished by and turned the corridor corner, the outgoing president's mindless shout of "wah, wah, wah, wah!" fading into the distance.

"Well," said Arthur Rodes, hitching at his trousers, and walking toward 911. "This is a nice place to visit. But I certainly wouldn't want to live here."

He won $216.

Arthur Rodes felt it was somewhat eerie, being spirited across the Florida peninsula in the early morning hours by a solemn, bearlike man wearing a three-cornered hat. Not a light was in sight, no sign of civilization. The straight highway lined out through its border of swamp. The whole world, seemingly, was empty of people.

Tipton asked suddenly, "Would you care for a martini?"

If he thinks I'm going to ask him where the hell he would find a martini out here, he's crazy, Art thought. He said, "No, not right now."

Cliff tilted back a milk bottle half full of gin.

Paul was snoring in the back seat. They had tried to wake him up but he kept asking where the bagpipes were. Eventually, they reached Flat City. Cliff gave Art instructions on how to get to the Higgins home and got out at the bus station.

"Glad to have met you, Art," he said. "I better go home now."

"Well, it's been interesting, Cliff."

From the bus depot at Guava Springs, Cliff Tipton caught a cab to his home. He had been gone several days. He said to his wife, "Mail these shoes to Paul Higgins, Flat City, O.K?"

"O.K."

Cliff ate some grapefruit, then went in and stared at his typewriter for three hours, and wrote a nasty note to the Acme Bakery again.

At the end of the three hours he threw the note in the waste-basket, walked out, tossed the three-cornered hat to Trudy and said, "Send this out and have it blocked."

"How can you block a triangular hat?"

"Oh, where's your sense of humor? That's the point—I throw you a three-cornered hat and say have it—"

"Did you like the place?"

"Boy, I sure did. It was so peaceful."

In Flat City Arthur Rodes was sleeping soundly. Betty was looking for her husband's shoes. Her husband was vainly trying to reconstruct the evening.

On Guava Springs Key, Cliff Tipton said, "I love peace."

CHAPTER FIFTEEN

A LITTLE BREEZE BLEW ACROSS the lake.

Paul and Art were sunning themselves on the raft. Lou and Tom Jedsoe were sunning themselves on the shore. Junior was digging worms. Betty was opening the box that came in the mail. It was a pair of Paul's shoes.

"This *is* a wonderful place," Art said, looking up at the sky, his arms folded under his head. "I see your point. I didn't know there was any place like it left. Maybe in two weeks I would be dying of boredom here, but right now I see your point. Not even a near neighbor to fight with."

"Tipton is going to move across the lake, or somewhere around here. Did I tell you?"

Art came up on one elbow. "What?"

"That's right," Paul said. "He's going to buy and build here. He likes over there where the big cypresses are, see? Where the river feeds in?"

"Is he serious?"

"Absolutely," Paul said, then noticed the look on Art's face. "What's with you?"

"Paul. Do you realize what it means if Tipton moves here?"

"Why, I suppose. Sure. Well have an occasional drink together. Our wives will talk, infrequently. I can't imagine a better neighbor. He's a nice guy—respects privacy. A very nice guy, crazy of course, and I better remember not to try to drink belt for belt with him, but—"

"Paul. Paul, Cliff Tipton is not just a nice guy."

"Well, I like him."

"Don't get offended. Think. This sun must be softening your head. He is not *just* a nice guy."

"Come again?"

"I'll give it to you in short takes. *Tipton is a world famous celebrity.* Had that occurred to you?"

"Well not particularly."

"No. Because you're getting clabber-headed. That crazy bastard is *famous!* If he moves here—wherever he moves—it will be *news.* It will be on every wire service. It will be in every column. And just what will be the first public reaction?"

Paul's eyes widened in alarm. " 'Where the hell is this Flat City anyhow?' "

"You're getting plugged back in. What will Earl Wilson say? 'Visited Tipton in charming tropical paradise.' What will Winchell say?"

" 'Tipton building Floridilly of a home down where flamingo means a bird,' " Paul muttered.

"Lyons will note that Toots Shor was telling Zsa Zsa that Alabama's Gov. Folsom told Howard Johnson that he envies Tipton's unspoiled paradise. And so on. I see by the mounting terror in your eyes you get the early pitch."

"My God," Paul said. "You're right."

"Paul, do you know how a resort area starts?"

A stricken Paul Higgins sat up and stared, hearing the shiny bulldozer.

"Oh, Paul, Paul," said Art Rodes sadly. "Even now it may be too late. What you needed was a good public relations man—rather a good *bad* public relations man."

"Let's go to work," Paul said. "We've got to unsell him."

"We will unsell him," Art Rodes said.

They waded ashore.

Side by side, in dripping trunks, they strode through the trees. Together, thus, they had roamed the asphalt canyons. Upstairs they sat, staring at one another across a desk made of planks lain across two sawhorses, instead of a desk made of mahogany. Paul went and got his peanut butter glass and filled it with sharpened yellow pencils and put it on the plank desk. Neither man spoke.

The hard unsell was born.

CHAPTER SIXTEEN

*While the term public relations did not
come into general use until after World
War I, many of its basic activities are as old
as history. Primitive priests and medicine
men performed public relations functions
on behalf of their tribes when, in order to
eliminate customs that were found to en-
danger the health or safety of the tribe, they
built bodies of legend to give sanctions to
their prohibitions.*

Public Relations
Encyclopædia Britannica

Aᴿᴱ ʏᴏᴜ ᴛᴡᴏ ᴄᴏᴍɪɴɢ ᴅᴏᴡɴ ꜰᴏʀ
supper or not?" Betty Higgins called up the stairs, the evening
of the afternoon the hard unsell of Flat County was born.

"Just send out for some sandwiches," her husband called
down. "I mean, just send up some sandwiches."

Paul was seated at the plank table in the upstairs bedroom they were using for an office. Art Rodes paced, in his bagging trunks, patting his bare chest where the cigar pocket should be.

Paul put his head in his hands. He said. "It can't be done."

"Don't hit the panic switch," Art said. "Just isolate the problem."

They had done the routine before, many times; working together, high above the streets of New York. They had been good propagandists, in a field where the mediocre died. Rodes-Higgins, the team, transplanted, now followed the same format; the Madison Avenue Boys in Flat County, mused Art Rodes as he paced. He said, "It is a twofold problem."

Paul groaned.

Art defined the problem: "How can Flat Country be kept as it is?"

Paul looked up with hopeless eyes and rattled his pencils in the glass.

Art asked, "What is the image we wish to create?"

A slight glint, the barest ray, came into Paul Higgins' eyes. He stood up. Both men paced, sans button-down shirts. The old piracy beat in the heart of Arthur Rodes and slowly the light of battle came to Paul's eyes. They talked. Bouncing it back and forth. Distilling it.

Art Rodes tacked a piece of copy paper on the wall and in big square letters penciled: "FLAT COUNTY IS A HORRIBLE PLACE TO LIVE."

They took a coffee break. Paul had a sudden strange yen to walk three blocks to a near-forgotten Groson's and have two martinis, the drink of communicative people.

Art said, "The problem has two main facets. We know the image we want to create. What audience do we wish to reach? First ask yourself, 'How does a resort area start?' "

He tacked up another piece of paper. On it he wrote: "CELEBRITY."

He penciled a box around it and said, "In this case, Tipton."

Then he wrote, "IMPRESSEES."

"What the hell does that mean?" Paul asked.

"People impressed by celebrities. The people who love to say, 'I could see Al Capone from my front porch.' The name-droppers who would love to say, 'My neighbor, Cliff Tipton, dropped by to kick the dog.' In this case, artistic impressees. The worst kind."

Paul nodded. The chart grew. Little squares joined by lines. Bohemians, hangers-on, opportunist merchants, *real estate men* —then the low-down-payment development, the friendly neighborhood shopping center, the works.

The completed formula read: "CELEBRITY *plus* IM-PRESSEES *plus* GOOD PUBLICITY = RESORT. ANTI-DOTE—BAD PUBLICITY."

"The formula is valid," Art said. "It's happened time and time again that a resort area starts just like this. All the elements—natural beauty—are here. The minute it is announced the famous Cliff Tipton has moved to a place called Flat County, it is on the way to happening! And fast."

"Oh, they'll move in, they'll move in," Paul groaned.

"Shhh. Steady. I'm right here with you."

"Lord, Lord, Lord," Paul said, despairingly.

"We've done it before, boy. Steady. Don't panic. We know our publics, our audiences."

"We know the image," Paul said hollowly.

"We know the problem."

"It is twofold." Paul said.

"The short range?"

"Keep that damn celebrity out of here."

"The long-range, Paul?"

Paul was pacing now. "Lay the groundwork to keep 'em *all* out of here. Write down snakes."

"What is our media? What publications do we try to hit?"

"Write down alligators," Paul said. "First we hit the local sheet and somehow get it picked up. Write down nematodes."

"You're working now, boy, you're working. How do you spell nematodes?"

"N-e-m-a-t-o-d-e-s. Write down poor economic investment."

"What *are* nematodes?"

"I'm not sure," Paul said impatiently. "They're bad, though. Write them down."

"What are you two *doing* up there?" Betty called, near midnight.

"Just send more coffee!" Paul shouted.

Late into the night they worked. The next day they did research, driving into Fort Myers. The following night they worked (and around the rim of the Golden Peninsula the forces of progress slept) and worked and worked. The problem had been isolated. Unsell Flat County to Tipton and the world —*and never let the client down.* Paul Higgins, at long last his own client, looked out on his land and lake in the moonlight: Thought of it overrun with outboards, resounding with yells and the bulldozers grunting at the tree boles.

"Wake up, Goddammit!" he snarled at Art Rodes. "It's early yet."

The following day they broached Editor Willingham.

Editor Theodore J. Willingham of the Flat City Ledger, Paul thought fearfully, can smell a press plant a mile—or twenty-five years—away, I am indeed afraid. Paul and Art, with innocent eyes, stood in the Ledger office, waiting for Willingham to read the copy slugged "For Immediate Release."

The old editor looked up from under his eyeshade. Then he looked back at the release they had handed him. He looked back at the copy. He looked up again. He spat on the floor.

He said, "I must be growing old and feeble. But I cannot find the angle. I can smell it, but I can't see it."

"Sir?" said Art, too innocently. But Willingham did not look at Art. He looked at Paul. Then he looked at the ceiling.

"I have walked with the righteous and the unrighteous," said

Theodore J. Willingham. "Good. I have known the lowly and the mighty. In the faraway cities I have toiled amidst wickedness and some of my worst friends have been press agents."

He spat. He said to the ceiling, "Little has escaped these rheumy eyes. Good. I have played poker the day before payday with Hearst copy-editors in a depression."

"Verily," said Pete Raney, the tall, wispy, old printer in his mighty deep voice, from the desk where he was reading proof, "and made book in New Orleans."

"But," said Mr. Willingham. "I cannot find the hole in this, I cannot ascertain the gimmick." He looked directly at Paul again. "Here," he said, "in this last stronghold of serenity, in my declining years, is a goddamn plant I cannot figure out."

He read it once more:

"The malaria rate in Flat County has declined sharply over the past few years, Florida State Health Department figures show, despite an as yet inadequate control of the dread female anopheles mosquito—the deadly malaria carrier."

Willingham nodded solemnly to himself. "Yes," he said. "That is true. Everybody used to have malaria and now nobody does. Indeed, a promising trend."

He leaned back and looked at Paul, this time with one sidelong glance at Art, and he said, "O.K., Paul. What is the pitch?"

Paul said wearily, "O.K., we'll level with you."

"Paul!" Art blurted, shocked. "Have you lost your mind?"

But Paul, while Art waggled his hands warningly, said to Willingham, "Mr. Willingham, do you want Flat County to turn into a resort area?"

"Now you've done it," Art hissed. "My God, how long have you been in this business, anyhow?"

"I see," Willingham said slowly, to Paul. "I see. Worried about them moving in on us, eh?"

"Exactly," Paul said.

"Smoke screen stuff, this?" Willingham said sourly, waving the paper.

"More or less," Paul admitted. "However, I—"

Willingham cut him off with a curt wave of his hand.

"Um." said Willingham.

Paul made a speech. He spoke of the beauties of nature. He was pro solitude and peace. He spoke at length. At length, he finished. Art, gamely leaping into what he considered a foreordained lost cause, took over.

"Anonymity has been your shield and buckler in this unspoiled nature's paradise," Art said. "What profiteth it a man if he—"

"Um," said Willingham. "Be back."

He walked out.

"We got a poet like you here," said Pete Raney, the printer, to Art. "He's the village idiot on the side."

"I hope Willingham didn't go for the sheriff," Paul groaned.

"Fine fellow," Raney said. "Does all his bookkeeping on the wall. Saves paperwork. Yuk, yunk, yunk."

They waited nearly fifteen minutes. Willingham returned, sat down at the rickety chair, spit on the floor and said, "Good. Now, Elroy McIntosh is a big factor. Owns practically all the land on the other side of the lake where Tipton would buy. He would sell his left buttock if the price was right."

Art's lower jaw sagged. Paul's face brightened. Paul said, "You're with us?"

"Been worried ever since I heard Tipton was visiting you. With you all the way. Didn't move here because I liked Coney Island. Used to live in Los Angeles. Hate tourists and may bohemians burn in hell. What other releases you got in your hand there, boy?"

"Oh," Art replied. "Little human interest stuff about alligators. A biography of the ground rattler pointing out that, although widely underfoot here, they are seldom fatal."

"A good postve note," Willingham said. "Matter of fact,

the diamond-backs won't kill you more'n fifty per cent of the time."

Art looked at him admiringly. "Tell me, good sir, were you ever a press agent?"

"Nope," said the editor. "Got a first cousin that was a con man for twenty years on the oceanliners, though. Arthur, don't ever try to snow an old trouper."

"Noted and done," said Art, happily. "Here's a little local economic study pointing out that while land values here are not exactly in the ascendancy like everyplace else in the world things may get better."

"Barring hurricanes," said Willingham. "Or freeze."

"We are working on nematodes," Paul said. "A little sketchy as yet, but it was a rush order."

"Nigger toes?" said Pete Raney. "Thought you was Yankees. It's Negro toes."

"I've been meaning to fire him for eighteen years," Willingham said. "You assumed, of course, that once I printed this stuff other papers would pick it up."

"It crossed our mind," Paul said.

"Well, in addition," the editor said, "we may have a good fast in to hit some pertinent papers for sure. There's a young fellow named Jerry Space who called me. His old man owns a bunch of papers down here. Jerry is coming through here. He's learning about Florida. He is very stupid. He is writing a series."

"I have died and gone to heaven," said Art Rodes.

Willingham took off his eyeshade. "One other thing," he said. "This town has no Chamber of Commerce, a lack I have never seen fit to utilize the power of the press to fill. However, as you may have considered, one drawback is the failure of these releases to quote an authoritative source."

Paul said, "We thought you might just use The Ledger learned this week sort of thing."

"Weak," Willingham said. "But I just went down and talked to the mayor. The mayor runs the dry goods store. He learned at an early age that if you buy pants in quantity, which is called wholesale, you get them at a low price. Then by selling them in smaller quantities, which is retail, in the technical nomenclature, you can jack the price to all the traffic will bear. This is all he knows and all he needs to know. Otherwise he is not a particularly perceptive man. He accepts your services."

"Our services?" said Art.

"Even our mayor wouldn't trust *you*," Willingham said kindly to Art. "Your services, Paul. He accepts them."

"The mayor? My services?"

Willingham shifted his chair around to face the Linotype keyboard, set type a little while, pulled a proof and handed it to Paul. Art read over his shoulder.

"Paul Higgins, new resident who is a former New York public relations consultant with wide newspaper and magazine writing experience, this week was named by the city to head the newly formed Flat City Publicity Bureau.

"The bureau, which has no formal office quarters, will create and handle publicity releases dealing with Flat City and the surrounding area, as well as provide tourist information when requested.

"Higgins, as head of the bureau, will receive no stipend and his duties are of a voluntary nature.

" 'We are indeed fortunate to secure the services of this topnotch man to handle this sadly overlooked facet of civic development, and Flat Citians are assured the new office will have my fullest cooperation and support,' said Mayor Elroy McIntosh, who made the appointment."

"Now," said Willingham, "we have an authoritative source to quote."

Arthur Rodes looked at Willingham in awe. Then he bowed low, in the deepest respect.

"Now," said Willingham, "We'll get started running this

stuff, but, specifically, how long will it be before Tipton comes down for another visit? Like to take him on a little tour. Does he like quicksand, do you know?"

"See," Paul said happily to Art. "Honesty *is* the best policy, even in public relations."

"That," said Art, "has always been my philosophy and my guide."

On Guava Springs Key that night the creative-type folk were being given another party by Rudolph Mace, book and drama editor of the Guava Springs Leader; a star in the cultural firmament. The old-timers usually went to Mace's parties, which weren't bad parties, right along with the younger creative-types who kept moving in, but they yearned for the old wild days.

Other old-timers, like Cliff Tipton, often thought of moving. They had seen their wilderness tamed and turned into, of all goddamn things, not only a resort but an "artists' colony." The young artists also bemoaned the situation they were helping to cause. Now everybody was drinking on the terraced lawn.

"Better a simple cabin away from all this than the distraction and cheapness all around us," said a young lady, a commercial artist, who supported her husband, a noncommercial artist. "Darling, I can't stand to see you stultified like this. I want to see you *paint, paint, paint!* I wonder where this place is Cliff Tipton keeps talking about? It's so *trite* here. Maybe we could move down in the same area. It sounds like such a *fun* place."

In Flat County the black lake lay silent, silent.

CHAPTER SEVENTEEN

MRS. PAUL HIGGINS, YOUNGISH matron formerly of fashionable Slathesdale, N.Y., where she had been active in school affairs and interested in charity, was bent over a washtub in her kitchen scrubbing a pair of jeans on a washboard before wrenching them out to dry.

She had a fine washer-dryer with an instrument panel like an airliner. It was out of whack. She was thinking that some enterprising washing machine firm might do well to enclose a washboard in each machine instead of a box of detergent. Inasmuch as washboards never got out of whack.

Her son was on the back porch putting the corpses of flies he had swatted into a bottle which had contained perfume.

"Cough," said a voice at the kitchen door. Betty turned. Two small tan boys were on the step. One said, "Is Fatback here?"

"What?"

"Fatback."

"Fatback?"

"Hi, fellows," Junior called. "Be right there."

He loaded a paper bag with potatoes.

"Are you going to have a cook-out, son?"

"Yes."

"That's nice. Be careful in the woods. What did that little boy call you?"

"Fatback. Because I didn't know what it was."

"Oh," Betty said. "What's in the bottle?"

"Dead flies," Junior said, and left.

Potatoes and dead flies. She thought it over at length. She reached no conclusion.

Actually, the potatoes were to put in swamp cabbage stew. The dead flies were to put in lizards. The flies and the lizards had no gastronomical connection with the stew. The lizards were to sell. There was a roadside animal show near Fort Myers that bought lizards, live and in good shape, for a dime each. Junior and his friends were postive of this. It was common knowledge. They had no idea why they were positive of it, but they were in the lizard business. They had 123 green lizards. They had a lizard cartel.

With his friends, Fatback Higgins walked firmly through the sandspurs. During the shirtless and shoeless weeks he had turned brown, tough: skinny sinew. He had been in four fights, averaging .500.

He lost the first two, which were caused by the fact he was a new boy. He won the third, sparked by a cracker lad's canard that the Yankees cheated in the War Between the States. By using mustard gas.

He also won the fourth, caused by Junior's sudden aversion to being called a Yankee. Now he didn't have to fight any more and instead of being nicknamed Yankee he was nicknamed Fatback. The point of his northern origin was forgotten, so he was no longer compelled to feel either proud or ashamed of it, one winning fight on each side of the issue being considered sufficient by even the most bigoted of his acquaintances.

These acquaintances were scattered. Flat County was sparsely populated. The lake section had few residents. But six boys lived in a reachable radius of each other.

Tim Monahan's father worked at the sawmill. Tim was popular because he was a local rarity, a Catholic, and had many tales of pagan rites. Furthermore he could lick the other five.

Arthur McIntosh was the son of the mayor. He was a weasel-faced lad of thirteen, acceptable because he quite often had considerable money, stolen from his father's cash register in the dry goods store. His father made him work there Friday nights and Saturdays because it was good training. Arthur added to his popularity by tearing down his father's "No Trespassing— Violators Will be Prosecuted" signs around his father's lake property and donating them to use as treehouse shingles.

Toby Neil, thirteen, had the most impressive qualifications. He was, he said, the son of Chief Orlando Flying Eagle, the famous Choctaw locomotive engineer and card sharp. Mrs. Neil, a seamstress, and a light in the Baptist church, would have been interested to hear this unique description of her late husband, who had been a surveyor for a railroad until he backed into a ravine, with his tripod, near Tulsa, Oklahoma, still sighting carefully through the telescope. Widowed, Mrs. Neil moved to Flat City where her brother had been in the smoked ham game.

"Toby gets his high cheekbones from his father," she often told her friends at the Wednesday circle. "Ebenezer had a little Indian blood, you know."

Another thing she often said was: "I'm as broad-minded as the next one, mind you, but I always say playing cards are the devil's handbills. No deck of cards will ever set foot in this house. That was poor Ebenezer's one fault. He insisted there was nothing wrong with playing cards."

Thus was born the bastard son of Flying Eagle. Toby, perhaps reverting to some nonfictional ancestor, did walk like a brave and was the best woodsman in the bunch.

Fatback first gained full acceptance merely by being the new boy and available for fighting, and as the son of the rich Yankee who typed a lot. He cemented his acceptance by telling various lies about the Northland and about the wild parties his folks had given. It was considered a bonus when Fatback volunteered to show the other boys how to hide behind the big century plant and watch his big sister and Tom Jedsoe in the front porch swing of an evening.

The Baldwin brothers, eleven and thirteen, were vague and quiet. Their father ran the feed store and sent them off to military school. They made no demands on anybody. Their father, who had been a first lieutenant in the Quartermaster Corps, felt that military school would make real men of them. They were obedient boys and minded well—not only their parents, but practically anybody with an authoritative snap in the voice.

Hammerhead Williams could make them do anything. Hammerhead—the sixth boy—was short, wiry and had perceptive eyes. His mother taught piano and believed in permissive child-rearing. His father was a dirt farmer who played the stock market. Hammerhead divided his time evenly between being allowed to give vent to his repressions and getting his fanny belted red for it. Once he stayed up in a tall turpentine pine for two days and a night until his father agreed to buy him a 12-gauge double-barreled shotgun. He had a mind of his own. So did his father, who broke the treaty when Hammerhead reached sea level, and whaled him good.

Hammerhead retaliated for the belting by making confetti of a $7.95 book on permissive child-rearing. His father locked him in the pantry, where he ate fifty stuffed olives and a jar of anchovy paste and shouted a nasty word. His father washed his mouth out with Pearlite, The Soap That Senses Your Skin Difficulties. Hammerhead's mother went home to her husband's mother under a prior arrangement, her own mother having passed away some years previously. They were reunited now, but Hammerhead was being kept home today as punishment for going back up in the pine tree.

The Baldwin brothers were also absent, having gone with their father to a patriotic function, a chicken fry sponsored by the American Legion to raise funds for a picnic.

Fatback, Toby, Tim and, particularly, Arthur McIntosh, did not overly mourn their absent comrades. Arthur pointed out the lizard profits would split better only four ways.

Arthur brought the stew meat and met the other three by the lizard cache on the river bank. They set about making swamp-cabbage stew. Swamp cabbage is heart of palm. Fatback Higgins was happy. He never thought of Slathesdale any more. There was too much here.

Junior had noticed his father in New York occasionally but it never occurred to him his father could do things like swimming or hunting or fishing.

Back in Slathesdale when the six-year-old set played family nobody wanted to be Daddy because nobody was sure what a daddy was supposed to do, Junior remembered that.

Now, at twelve, Junior was astonished to find his father knew a great many things. And was losing his fat belly.

Back in Slathesdale the sissies who came to see his sister were just creeps who wouldn't do much even when you tied their shoelaces together so they would fall on their ass when they got up. Here, however, only yesterday evening, Tom Jedsoe had caught him behind the century plant and shook him until his eyeballs rattled. It gave a boy a feeling of security.

At the clearing the boys boiled and ate the stew. They waited ten minutes to avoid cramps then went swimming. They went naked and dripping to the lizard cache. A homemade box of screening and lathes held a mass of live lizards. Fatback dumped in the flies. Thunder sounded.

Toby said, "It's going to rain like hell."

Arthur McIntosh said, "We can't leave them here."

The skies were black and glowering when the boys went

home. Fatback had the lizards. He was a committee of one to guard them. He scooted up the stairs to the bedroom where nobody slept. Carefully, he shoved the box of lizards well back under the bed. Sometimes parents were funny about lizards.

Downstairs, somebody was knocking on the front wall.

Jerry Space stood on the porch, sweating in his Palm Beach suit, an ivory-tipped cigarette hanging from the corner of his mouth. He peered closely at the wall where the door should be.

"What the hell kind of a place is this?" he half-whimpered, pounding on the wall. He had heard, vaguely, that it used to belong to one of his uncles but he had never been in Flat County before.

He would have been perfectly contented to keep it that way. His heart was not really in his work.

Old Willingham was a part-time correspondent for his father's papers and had been suggested to him as a source. Willingham, in turn, had given him directions to the Publicity Bureau and promised to meet him right after office hours.

Jerry's father had delivered the ultimatum. No more stalling. Do a bang-up job of interpreting Florida. Or else.

If I had known he was really going to make me work, Jerry thought, I would have tried one more school. He pounded angrily on the blank wall.

"Don't knock the wall down," said a low voice.

He turned and looked at the vision. Her arms were firm and brown and her legs, in the shorts, were firm and brown and her hair was long and black. Her eyes were large and warm. She was smiling at him. She was trying to tell him something.

"Around the side here."

He identified himself, holding the vision's hand so it wouldn't go away. He felt a disturbing influence at work. It was to the right. It was human, a large human, a male, a very large male. It was trying to tell him something.

"I'm Tom Jedsoe."

"Oog," grunted Jerry as the large male squashed his hand.

Another large, but older male came striding around the house and said, "Well. You must be Jerry Space. Mr. Willingham called. So happy to meet you."

And a Mr. Rodes seemed delighted to see him. And when Mr. Willingham got out *he* seemed delighted to see him all over again. The natives certainly are friendly, Jerry thought. I had heard these rural types were like that.

It was an excellent dinner, although Jerry usually detested Southern cooking. He complimented Mrs. Higgins on her cornbread and snap beans and she curtsied.

"Wal," said Mr. Rodes. "What say us menfolks adjern to the parlor?"

"Now, Jerry," Willingham said. "Why don't you tell these folks just what you have in mind?"

"Well," said Jerry. "I'm sort of doing this series and it's sort of hard to explain."

"You mean capturing the *spirit* of Florida?" said Mr. Rodes and after a few minutes Jerry felt he had explained it all very well, and was gratified—he hadn't actually understood it himself previously.

He basked under the admiring eyes of the three men he was explaining it to. "The Space papers cover Florida like the sunshine," he said, and they seemed impressed.

"You'll stay over, of course," Higgins said.

"Oh, I don't know," Jerry said, looking at his watch. The vision in shorts went by the door, lugging dirty dishes. She smiled at him.

"Well . . ." Jerry said, "if you insist."

They insisted. They were very friendly.

"Do you find newspaper work interesting?" the girl, named Lou, asked when she came in from the kitchen.

"Fascinating," said Jerry, staring at her.

Arthur, handing Jerry another highball, pulled Lou into the kitchen. She didn't come back.

Later, Betty Higgins, wiping her hands on her apron, came in and sat down and said: "Well, how do you like the newspaper business?"

"It's O.K.," he said, still watching the door hopefully.

Paul leaped up, handed Jerry another highball, and pulled Betty into the kitchen. She didn't come back either.

But the men told him lots of helpful things.

When he got sleepy, Paul showed him his bed.

It was the bed in the guest room. The bed with 123 lizards under it.

In the great mystery of life one thing is certain: There's one in every crowd. This one follows not the norm nor heeds the precedent. He takes nothing for granted. He is the change-bringer.

He watched the bulky sledges drug and thought there must be an easier way: the wheel. He got tired of shivering: Portable fire. He got tired of beating his apparel on a flat rock: the washer-dryer.

Of the 123 lizards dwelling in the Higgins home, unknown to all but Junior, 122 were defeatists; victims of the herd instinct, livers of lives of quiet desperation.

The 123rd had the spark.

Maybe the spirit of a reincarnated Spanish explorer beat in his palpitating breast. Maybe he didn't like Arpège-flavored houseflies. Whatever his reason, he found—by standing on his tiptoes—the one ripped hole in the screened box surrounding him on all sides.

"Hssst, fellows," he whispered, pointing, kicking his tribe-mates awake. "Looky."

"That Larry!" the other lizards said. "Just leave it to him!"

"He has a keen mind," the other lizards, coming awake, said. "Tempermental, yes, and a poor credit risk. But touched with occasional brillance."

"Sh. You'll wake the warden."

The dawn was still distant as the lizards began to emerge,

their little pointy heads turning this way and that; some went hither, some went yon.

The old house was quiet in the dark. Mr. and Mrs. Higgins slept downstairs. Art Rodes slept in the bedroom which doubled as the Publicity Bureau.

In the adjoining room slept Fatback Higgins. Down the upstairs hall and across it Miss Lou Higgins snored delicately, half smiling, the glint of a moonbeam on her cheek. But of all these rooms the lizards had to stay in Jerry's, because the door was closed.

Jerry was dreaming of a land where all the men's room doors were locked. He struggled to stay asleep but nature called louder. They had switched to beer when the bourbon ran out, in the midst of a discussion of economic conditions in south central Florida.

(He had taken notes: "Always darkest before dawn and barring another crop failure hard-scrabbling farmers this section may recoup losses if can raise capital for soil enrichment. Keeping chins up.")

Jerry moved around in the bed, finally came awake, facing reality. He swung his feet out of bed, got up in the blackness. Carefully, he walked full into a wall. Something seemed to brush first one bare foot, then the other. He began, in his half-awakeness, to want the light switch very badly. He had heard enough about snakes for one night.

He found the switch. He switched on the light.

A green lizard was on the wall, looking at him.

He took a step back. A lizard climbed his instep. "Woo!" he said, and did a little dance. A lizard ran across his other foot. He increased the dance tempo.

"No," he said warningly, coming awake now. "No. No, now."

But it was not a dream. Surely enough, he was dancing about in a million lizards. He could see that. A house didn't have to fall on him.

He screamed a heartfelt scream and dashed from this hell

not of his making, ran blindly as the forest pig fleeing the boa and plunging down the hallway he shouted one more mighty shout, stumbled and fell headlong against a door which opened.

Lou Higgins sat straight up in bed.

She saw, in the light pouring through the door from the hall, a man clad only in shorts and flapping his arms and leaping about announcing, "Gotaboutagoddamn! Whooga whooga!"

She screamed her head off. Up the stairs Paul Higgins sped with a ballbat. From his room raced Arthur Rodes waving a badminton racket with no strings in it. Downstairs Betty Higgins was being thrown to her knees by stumbling over the hem of her husband's bathrobe she had put on in the dark. Even Junior woke up.

"All over!" Jerry shouted, executing a mighty leap as he discovered a lizard in the seat of his drawers. "Everywhere. *OH MY GOD!*"

Slowly, they calmed Jerry down. They told Lou and Junior to go back to sleep. They looked in Jerry's room.

"See?" he babbled. "See, see, see, see?"

"Holy mackerel," Paul said. "Look at all the lizards."

Now, public relations is an ad-lib art, so when Arthur Rodes looked in at a room thick with green lizards he merely said, "Oh, Jerry, didn't we tell you about the lizards?"

Junior, racing up, shouted in dismay after one look: "Hey! Who let all—UGGG."

Art clasped a hand over Junior's mouth and lugged him back to his room. Junior was choking, aggle, aggle. Art went in Junior's room with him and in a very short time there was the quiet which always accompanies bribery.

"Tell me about the lizards?" Jerry kept saying, in the quiet which often precedes hysteria. "Tell me *what* about the lizards? What? What?"

"Uh," Paul said. "We'll tell you all about the lizards tomorrow. Now you need sleep. Sleep downstairs on the sofa. The, ah, lizards never go in the living room."

Numbly, dumbly, Jerry put on a pair of Paul's pajamas and, as instructed, lay down on the couch in the dark living room. It is always darkest before the dawn.

Upstairs in Rodes-Higgins, Arthur said: "I would say the invasion came in from the dry Tortugas."

The head of the Flat City Publicity Bureau said: "Their bite is not believed to be fatal or even dangerous if ordinary antiseptic measures are taken."

Art said: "Verification of this is expected from a herpetologist to whom several of the larger specimans have been sent."

"Yes. Expected in the near future. Actually, in nature's plan —strike that. Read it actually in the wondrous *balance of nature* these somewhat loathsome creatures serve a useful purpose, your correspondent learned."

"They eat nematodes."

"No. But they do help to destroy the deadly malaria carrier, the female anopheles mosquito."

"So thick in this area."

"Thus doth Mother Nature protect her children in Flat County, Florida."

"If the malaria don't get you the reptiles will."

"Let's go to bed," Paul said.

"A job well done," said Art. "I'll tell you about Junior's payoff later. Did you know he was in the lizard business?"

"No. Anyhow, this should make Jerry a bright little story for his daddy's papers tomorrow."

"Daddy will be proud of him."

Downstairs on the couch lay Jerry Space, stiffly, rigidly, waiting to hear rustlings on the floor, his eyes protruding like a hoptoad's. He did not dare go to the bathroom.

CHAPTER EIGHTEEN

THE DAWN OF THE MORNING after the lizards was cool and smelled of more rain coming. Paul was up early, watching the sun come up, walking the banks of his lake; the quietness all around him. His bare feet squished through the grass—he moved slowly along the water's edge, wearing only bathing trunks, by himself, thinking, tasting the morning.

The orange dawn glinted on the solemn lake and a heron stood in the grass by the shore near a cypress bole; waiting for minnows.

The hard unsell was no joke with Paul Higgins. He took it very seriously. He knew it would work, given only time. He reached for a cigarette in the pack at his waist band, but decided instead to smell the morning. The freshness each day still surprised him, and, once in a while, he still woke up wondering if he would have to rush to catch the train to the buildings.

God! he thought, how glad I am that I don't. He skimmed a rock across the lake. It bounced four times.

The book was going all right, off and on. Of the five short stories he had written three had been accepted, two rejected, and he was working on a sixth. He had met expenses, to his utter astonishment; he had made Betty check the accounts three times, but it was true.

What a strange feeling to be happy, he thought. The lake lapped silently. He thought of it loud with people.

If they ever start, he thought, they'll come like red ants. . . .

He felt a wave of rage and knew how the conquered must feel when the invaders march in. He turned and walked back toward his house lighting a Kool, which brand he smoked on his private theory that menthol probably helped lung cancer.

Suppose I *did* die of something, he thought, as I very well might, because I am forty-five—suppose I did die, next step. I've got a home and money in the bank and stocks and I'm up to my ass in insurance. Why if I died this very minute my family would be well taken care of. The thought of dying under such virtuous circumstances cheered him immensely and he whistled up the path.

Betty was making coffee and Jerry Space stumbled down from the bathroom.

"Did you sleep, after all that?" Betty asked Jerry.

"So so," Jerry mumbled. He sipped his coffee and said plaintively to Betty, "Explain the lizards to me."

"Art will explain right after breakfast, Jerry," Paul said hastily. And Art did.

That afternoon Art Rodes got Lou to run him into Flat City where he sat in Snooker Charley's Pool Parlor and Lending Library, on the main street, watching the police chief and Snooker Charley shooting nine-ball for two-bits a game.

Art chuckled, thinking of Jerry and the lizards. Paul still had Jerry out at the house, filling him in on Flat County. The lizard story, Art thought, should be a dilly in itself. Mysterious on-slaught . . . invasion puzzles.

Art felt good. The restful time he had spent in Flat City had been unique in his experience. And he took pride in the material he had helped prepare for the Flat City Ledger. Three stories had already run. A nice scrapbook was building up. Jerry Space would be a windfall. (Mentally, Art filed away the Space publications for use in behalf of his New York clients in the future.) The hard unsell was making great progress.

Maybe, Art thought, I can work up an article on the female anopheles and sell it to the Atlantic, thereby working in Creation's chemical insecticide client, also.

He watched Snooker bank the nine-ball in on a nice two-railer, while the police chief frowned. Art got up and wandered over to the bookshelves in the front of the poolroom. He thumbed through a volume titled Scarlet Sin at Sunrise, noting it formerly had been titled Unplumbed Heights. He looked at the picture of the author on the jacket. The author had on a turtle-neck sweater and obviously had been torn by life. He read the jacket blurb. "Before turning novelist," he read, "young Snidley had been a former police reporter and held a weird assortment of jobs, including working as a cumquat harvester and at one point holding a job as tester in a pressure-canned whipped-cream factory. In this, his first novel, he has captured the passion and turmoil rampant among the devil-may-care breed of crop-dusters and their women who wait, scanning the horizon for the tiny planes and the men who fly them—pawns in a game of destiny aloft."

"Had been a former police reporter?" Art thought.

Art was an expert on book jackets. Once on a paper he had been the chief book reviewer. There was no extra pay for this but you got to keep the review copy, which could be sold cheap to the local bookstores. Art's average for the course was an eight-paragraph review in ten minutes. He had, in a pinch before payday, reviewed as many as ten books an hour. He got the plot off the jacket, a sample paragraph at random. "Although Wallington has a natural feel for language," he would write, "occasionally his rhetoric runs away unbridled. Take, for instance, his passage concerning . . ." At this point Art would rapidly flip open the book, copy the first paragraph his eye fell on, wind up the review in a vaguely complimentary manner, comparing the author to the early John J. Newland or Wellston Sinclair before Sinclair turned cosmic. The fact that a large percentage of the names he used were made up on the spur of the moment brought no comment from anybody, and he had reviewed hundreds of books in that manner. Art himself later became John J. Newland, a nom de plume he used for his more outrageous effusions to further various clients' interests. Art often thought of himself as the early John J. Newland.

He poked his head out the front door and looked down the street but Paul was nowhere in sight.

They were going to take Junior to the animal man over near Fort Myers this afternoon. That was part of the payoff for Junior's keeping his mouth shut. Art, in Junior's room while Jerry had been leaping about during the lizard scare, had contracted to buy the current crop of lizards—had been forced also to agree that he and Paul would take Junior and his friend Toby over to dicker with the animal man rumored to buy lizards.

"Why would anybody buy lizards?" Art had demanded.

"They're not lizards, they're chameleons, everybody knows that, and they sell them for souvenirs and everybody says the man will buy them and we're going into business and—"

"All right, all right. Shhh."

Art put the book back on the shelf.

James A. Wedley was writing a book. Arthur grinned sardonically, thinking of the letter he had gotten from Otto Anvel yesterday: "Wedley," Otto had said, "is now an aspiring author. I believe he is going to expose Madison Avenue. It is a wonder somebody hasn't thought of this before."

Walking over to the cooler, Art opened himself a bottle of

beer, ambled back to the lending library area. He had asked
Snooker how a poolroom happened to incorporate a library.
"I don't know," Snooker had replied. "It was here when I
bought the place." This must be the only poolroom in the
world, Art mused, which has four copies of The Power of
Positive Thinking next to a nude calendar.

"Shoot!" Snooker Charley barked, just as Chief Williams
started to shoot. Williams scratched into the side pocket, and
threw his cuestick against the wall.

"Damn you to hell, Snooker!" Chief Williams shouted. "You
do that one more time and I'll close this place down!"

"Do what?" Snooker asked innocently.

"Dirty pool!" the police chief screamed.

"Say which?"

"I'm four bucks in the hole and you pull that," Williams
breathed, panting. "Damn it to hell, I'll close you down. We
got gambling laws in this town, you know."

"Begging your humble pardon," said Snooker, and sank the
nine-ball in the corner.

A big black car zoomed fast down Main.

"Hey Lordy!" shouted Chief Williams, dropping his cue.
"There goes one now." He ran out the door toward his law
enforcement vehicle.

Snooker watched him go. "Don't know what he would do
without them once-in-a-while Yankees," he said. "I swear, if I
didn't know him better I'd swear he turns the road signs around."

Snooker then smiled a gentle smile and said, "Well, I hope
he catches 'em. I can use the fine money. Got to buy my crazy
brother some atabrine."

"Atabrine?" Art said. "You mean he has malaria?"

"Oh, hell no, he ain't got nothing. But he thinks he's got
malaria. The stupid bastard. Come down with it the very day
after old Willingham started them malaria stories. About them
mosquitoes. My brother been et up by mosquitoes for his thirty-
five years but two of them stories put him flat on his back."

"Any other cases?" Art asked hopefully.

"Naw. But Billy Joe reads fast. One thing. The malaria cured his fat blood he was worrying about. He got that out of one of them little magazines about what you get every month. Like syphilis. Billy Joe swore he had syphilis for years around here on account of them magazines. Thought he never would get rid of that but along came all them stories on corty-sone, so he forgot about his syphilis and got arthritis."

"I'm a gall bladder man, myself," Art said.

"Shoot you double or nothing for that beer," Snooker said hopefully."

"Oh, no, you don't," Art said. "Say, how did you come by all these copies of the Gideon Bible?"

"A drummer named O'Kean used to bring me a few every year. He said he was a vice president in an organization what took Bibles out of hotel rooms."

"They lend a certain spiritual quality."

"Say which?"

"I say it's a Good Book."

"I seen the movie. Tell you what. I'll spot you the eight-ball and shoot you for the beer, double or nothing."

"Oh well, it's the only game in town," Art said. As he selected a cue, he heard the car outside honking. "Some other time, Snooker," he said. "Here's Paul."

Junior and the boy named Toby Neil were in the back seat. Art climbed in front with Paul. As the Higgins car moved off down Main street it met the police car coming back.

"Get him?" Art called, leaning out.

"Like a duck on a June bug!" Chief Williams shouted.

Settling back for the long drive, Art said, "The people around here are exceedingly well adjusted."

Paul Senior said, "This is a wild duck chase. Goose chase. The only animal show anybody knows anything about is twenty miles north of Fort Myers. You know they wouldn't buy lizards."

"You promised," Junior said. "And they aren't lizards. They're chameleons. You promised."

"Where is the ace reporter?" Art asked Paul. "Ace Space?"

"Swimming with Lou," Paul said, "And bucking for a fat lip, if I correctly decipher that gleam in Tom Jedsoe's eye."

Paul watched the flatlands of Florida through Air Force sunglasses. The city limits sign was nearly five miles out. Chief Williams liked a large arena. YOU ARE NOW LEAVING FRIENDLY FLAT CITY, said the billboard. On the other side it said, YOU ARE NOW ENTERING FRIENDLY FLAT CITY.

One speeder, a bicycle manufacturer from St. Louis, a man with a sense of that fine line which separates reality from hallucination, looked into his rear view mirror one day in this deserted land. He saw a huge black automobile pursuing him. The St. Louisan, on being informed he was doing seventy in a twenty-five-mile zone inside the city limits, looked around the empty terrain for some sign of civilization, something to cling to in a changing world. But there was only the prairieland and the white-sprayed sky.

"Fine little town you got here," the tourist had said to the police officer. "What is it? Oz?"

Passing the city limits of Flat City, Paul drove fast, looking approvingly at what he saw. He loved the unmarred greenness and the almost unreal emptiness, the pines stark against the far horizon. No car met him and no car passed. The emptiness satisfied a deep need, the quiet soothed nerves which had heard too much jangle too long. He loved this place, at the same time understanding how it could look bleak to others. He knew, for instance, that the flatness was merely boring to Art.

Buzzards hovered. A possum was dead by the roadside. It was a place of silence, Flat County. Man had never been officially recognized here. This was still as it had been. The asphalt was merely a thin line across time. Quail rose suddenly, a half dozen; a machine noise against the quietness as they fluttered. At night the frogs croaked.

The change came abruptly, not very far from the Gulf and the coastal highway. The narrow asphalt road came into a highway—two glaringly white filling stations of opposing oil companies glowered catty-cornered at one another where the roads crossed.

Each station—one was white and one was blue—was long, low and sterile, each a creation of an imagination shaped like a cookie cutter. On the third corner was a long, low motel. On the fourth corner, painted a stomach-churning orange, was an emporium which sold root beer and pizza-pups, which were wienies wrapped in small tomato pizzas and decorated with anchovies and a hidden plastic toothpick for the roof of your mouth.

The local industrial development committee had high hopes of interesting a Cleveland firm in putting in a branch safety pin factory in the area. It was a fast-growing and progressive area. It was about fifty miles west of Flat City. It was the perimeter. The light at the intersection was yellow on all four sides.

An old redbone hound, veteran of many hunts, walked feebly by the side of the highway, his eyes nearly blind, the dry palmettoes rustling, already tuning up for his requiem, this veteran of many other journeys. He walked across the highway and was almost hit by a car; he had forgotten another road had come where all the scents used to be.

A big yellow dirt-mover was golden in the sun. In the cab of the yellow machine sat a man with a face like a Viking, sweltering two miles from—but forever lost to—the spraying sea. He wiped his brow with a red bandanna, and the blade bit in. Once he had found an arrowhead and taken it to his son.

The machine strained and the topsoil moved and the coral was white as bone, unpleasantly glaring.

The refrigerated trucks roared north. The shiny cars roared too, both ways, wheeling past one another, going to or coming from Florida. All the engines of all the machines grated in one big snarl. There was a traffic tieup on the bridge north of Fort Myers.

There were signs.

SHELLS! DON'T FORGET YOUR
FRIENDS BACK HOME

All up and down the trail were signs.

SEE THE MONSTER GATORS

There was much progress everywhere and people en route to look at Seminole Indians commented on it.

PRALINES!

You could buy land for a small down payment. For only $25 down per lot (minimum of two lots to a customer) you could buy part of the planet Earth and it would be yours in Sunny Florida.

Of course, you didn't have the change of the seasons.

"See?" said Paul. "See?"

"Sure, I see," Art said. "You know what this will be?"

"One big Miami."

"Worse. One big Los Angeles."

The coast of west Florida pulsated with progress and pushed against the perimeter, came up to an intersection where—back toward Flat County—a blacktop road ran off into what appeared to be nowhere. But progress was seeking its own level. The crowds continued to come.

"If it ever occurs to just one promoter—" Paul said grimly.

"You're safe. For a long while. The pickings are too ripe over here on the coast. Play it like we're playing it. You're safe for a while. You can con Tipton out of his impulse to move down."

"I don't know," Paul said, doubtfully. "He really was hit hard by the place."

"He may have forgotten it already. You know how those writer-types are."

"I don't know," Paul said. "He's a pretty angry man about what's happening to his coast."

"Don't worry," Art said soothingly. "Simply don't worry."

"He loved the lake so."

"The contaminated one? Or the one with the water moccasins in it?"

"Hey," Paul said. "That must be it."

HIPPO HANNEGAN'S HIPPODROME

The large, faded, ripped canvas banner fluttered over a tall board fence facing the highway. On the fence were painted promises. SEE FAMOUS DANCING BEARS. SEE MONSTER GATORS. SEE MAN EATING FELINES. SEE RAPACIOUS REPTILES.

It was a roadside animal pitch like a hundred others in Florida, except sleazier looking.

FREE FREE FREE

They parked and walked in through the open gate. Nobody was around. Directly inside the gate was a little turnstile, broken. A sign stated that the great entertainment and educational enterprise was dependent on voluntary contributions.

Paul dropped some coins into the plate on the turnstile. Inside they could see no one. In a shallow, wired-over pit a few snakes lay asleep. In another pit two alligators were asleep. The grass inside the clearing was badly in need of cutting. A dilapidated hammock was strung between two pine trees and an alley cat was asleep in it. There were a few cages with mouldy-looking animals in them: A couple of coyotes, two bobcats, an armadillo. What seemed to be the star attraction was housed in a separate tent which carried the legend: FAMOUS RUSSIAN DANCING BEARS. Plus a second sign stressing the point that donations would not be amiss.

It was Junior who found Hippo Hannegan.

The proprietor of this galaxy of entertainment was asleep in the backseat of a 1940 Hudson hard by the souvenir stand. Junior aroused him by shouting in his ear, "Do you buy chameleons?"

The man sat up, his eyes wild.

Seeing human visitors, he clambered swiftly out of his resting place, kicking open a stuck door. He bustled about in little circles, obviously astonished to meet his fellow men here. He looked like Robinson Crusoe finding the footprint.

"Good morning, good morning," he said over and over, although it was three in the afternoon. "Shell bracelets? Don't forget the folks back home."

"We—" said Paul.

"Don't miss the dancing bears!" the proprietor said, still circling, still not quite awake.

"Do—" said Junior.

"I have some wonderful mother-of-pearl necklaces!"

"Do you buy chameleons?" demanded Toby Neil.

"Do I what?"

"Mr. Hannegan?" Paul broke in. The man nodded. Paul said, "Somebody told the kids you bought chameleons. Lizards. And they catch them. Sorry to bother you. You don't buy lizards, do you?"

Hippo Hannegan began to gain a little more speed as he walked back and forth, circling slightly. He stretched his arms to the skies, speaking to his deity, not to his visitors. He was a short, thin man with a long nose and an astonishing mop of red hair. He looked like an angry elf in need of a haircut.

Hippo Hannegan began to walk in little circles, talking to unseen listeners.

"Buy lizards?" he said. "No. No." He said it quietly. "No, I don't buy lizards. I buy junk bears from a thief brother-in-law. I leave a good job in Fresno to come to Florida and make my fortune. I am buying a bobcat with the sleeping sickness. But buy lizards? No. My friend, I tell you this. I do not buy lizards. This is the one exception in a life of stupidity. I wouldn't buy a lizard if you paid me to."

"He doesn't buy lizards," Art said to Junior.

"Well," Junior said. "As long as we're here, I would like to see the dancing bears."

Hannegan brightened. He picked up a hoe handle and dashed

into the bear tent. "Up, up, everybody up!" they heard him shouting, his voice accompanied by the sound of mighty thacks. "Up, you dumbo bastards. We got company. Put on your hats and dance!"

They learned two things about Hippo Hannegan: One he was not so named for his size, but short for Hippocrates. His father had wanted him to be a veterinarian. Secondly, the reason for his habit of walking in little circles was the dancing bears. They really didn't like to dance and Hippo had to get in the arena with them. And Hippo led.

CHAPTER NINETEEN

Harrington space had declared a half holiday for most employees of the Guava Springs Leader. That's how momentous an occasion it was.

The dedication of the beautiful new Progress Tower was to be at 3 p.m. There would be a guided tour. Top executives from throughout the Space empire would be on hand, along with many prominent personages. There would be the unveiling of the beautiful Message of Progress on which the stonecutter had labored furiously, meeting the deadline in the best journalistic tradition.

Harrington Space was in an expansive mood. He puffed happily around his office. He looked approvingly at the page-one feature by Gerald Space, All-Florida correspondent. It was about the excellent work being done in rattlesnake control in a place called Flat County. It was very readable and was running in all the Space papers as part of the series. People liked to read about rattlesnakes.

The boy was doing a great job. Everybody said so. He showed unsuspected talent in both writing and research, and had a good feature touch too. The piece he had sent in last Saturday, about the strange invasion of lizards in south central Florida, fairly sang. People liked to read about lizards.

Upcoming now was his piece about the agricultural picture in south central Florida. It was as interpretative as one could ask. They were doing valiant battle against heavy odds down there, those lean and tight-lipped tillers of the soil; fighting the deadly nematode, despite inadequate highways.

Hmm, Harrington thought. He jotted down a memo to himself: "See if own any property around place called Flat County and unload soonest."

Yessir, he thought happily, I knew that boy had it in him —it just needed the right assignment to bring it out. I'm glad, Harrington mused, that I sent him out to learn the interpretative end of the business.

Harrington looked at himself in the wall mirror, turning his profile slightly. A great editor, he thought, comes along how often? Ten years? Twenty? Once in a lifetime?

It was shortly after the noon hour. A festive air filled the town, Harrington was certain, as the dedication time approached. How eager the employees must be to move into their new quarters!

The newspaper operation would not move into the new headquarters tower for a few weeks yet, but Harrington knew his employees lived in wild anticipation of the event.

In this he was slightly mistaken. To a man, they would have settled for a $7.50 raise.

Downstairs, the city room, the offices of Floridawide Magazine and all the various departments which dealt with the Space syndicate operations were empty, except for a skeleton staff.

An elderly editorial writer, who hadn't gotten word of the holiday, nevertheless sniffed something of a holiday nature in the air and instinctively sat down and wrote a Labor Day editorial urging safe driving. ("Stop this senseless slaughter!")

The slot man—disgruntled at being kept on as part of the skeleton crew—was conscientiously belting the fifth of Gilbey's Gin hidden in the towel rack. By two o'clock he was trying to look up the definition of nematode in the city directory, until a helpful underling handed him the telephone book instead. By that time he had forgotten what he was doing anyway and the copy went down the chute. Then he, too, departed. The office was deserted, except for the editorial writer who was constructing an essay urging water safety. ("Don't be a statistic!")

Upstairs in the executive offices, Harrington received the mayor. He received the representative from the gubernatorial office in Tallahassee. He received inspirational wires of congratulation. The secretary of the Chamber of Commerce said Harrington was the Roy Howard of the Sunshine State. Harrington held what he called a little get-together shortly before the assembly moved down to the new tower for the dedication.

Harrington himself conducted the guided preview tour of Progress Tower for this prominent assembly. Then everybody convened in Harrington's new office at the tower.

Shortly before 3 o'clock Clifton Tipton, his upper left arm grasped firmly by his wife, was dragged in and greeted enthusiastically. The lady president of the Croton Club got his autograph. Tipton leaned glumly on the bar. Mrs. Tipton got him a drink. It was water. He had promised. He put some olives in his water.

Top executives milled about putting their best feet forward. *Harrington*, they said, *that's a bang-up good job Jer is doing!* Their wives counted their trips to the bar.

Ricky,· the executive editor, ran frantically up to the roof and back repeatedly, sweating through his Dacron, clutching at his bow tie. The weather ball was flashing rain and colder although the skies were clear and blistering.

A young reporter, hated by his city editor because he had

gone one year to Harvard, ran around like a crazed turkey, scared to death because he had caught the dread dedication-story assignment, Old Balloon-Ass's platinum-plated brainstorm. In newspapering all stories having anything to do with the publisher come out wrong.

"Plaid wastebskts," the reporter wrote incoherently on his copy paper, taking voluminous notes, later losing them en route back to the Leader office. "Lots glass windows. People. Rntt eddlpln."

The old photographer with him, chewing his cud and trying to remember parlay odds at the Tampa dog track, handed the esteemed Harrington (Balloon-Ass) Space a piece of paper and said, "Here, Chief. Hold this and look like you're thinking. Quit mugging the camera. That's it. One more."

"A good man," Harrington said to the franchise holder for an important catsup concern. "A real old school photographer. He has printer's ink in his veins." Harrington turned to the reporter, who was taking notes about the rug-to-rug walls, and said abruptly, "You there!"

"Oof!" said the Harvard man, leaping goatlike into the air, startled.

"Getting everything you need, son?" the great publisher inquired kindly.

"Yes see!" the reporter shouted. "I mean, See sir!"

Harrington looked at the modernistic wall clock, trying to figure out what time it was. Finally, he gave up and looked at his watch. He said, "Well, folks, the time has come!"

"Thank a merciful God," said glum voice from near the bar.

Downstairs went the assembly, admiring everything en route. Ricky passed them on his scurrying way back to the roof. The commoners awaited outside near the entrance where the speakers' platform had been put up. Open house was to follow.

Various people spoke. They spoke of what Progress Tower would mean to the city, state and nation. The mayor spoke.

The prominent writer, Mr. Tipton, got up and then sat down, to wild applause. Then a man introduced a man who introduced a man who said Harrington Space needed no introduction.

Harrington folded his hands across his tummy and said in his deepest voice that this was indeed a red-letter day.

"But how far better than mere words," he said, "is this inspiring message in stone, hewn like granite to say to the future generations of coming posterity to follow, "Progress begins at home!"

"Indeed," he said, "how privileged we are to have such a great writer as Clifton Tipton in our midst, to contribute a thought which will ring down through the ages of the Sunshine State like a flag unfurled, bespeaking a noble sentiment toward what, we, ah, as we stand here today!"

The man was ready to pull the rope to unveil the message carved on the façade over the entrance to Progress Tower.

"Unveil the message to future posterity!" Harrington Space shouted, and the bright-hued cloth fell away. The vast assembly looked up at it, some moving their lips.

PROGRESS

Progress . . .
Without progress there
Can be
No advancement . . .

Progress?
Forward! For to progress one
Must inevitably move
Forward, else lose the name
Of Progress . . .

Progress!
Nor faintly query how!

By sharp prow
Forward and with stern
Arear—well tillered . . .

Progress,
Ahead. And with full-throated
Cry, sharp as this lofty and speared
Spire, pointing the sun,
All hail the forwardness of
F R O G R E S S !

There on the façade of Progress Tower, this lofty and speared spire, was the first stone-carved typographical error in the glorious history of journalism.

"Frogress?" said the Harvard Man. "Frogress?"

From the speakers' platform the laughter of Cliff Tipton rose like a manic loon.

From the crowd an old wire service reporter shouted his battle cry, "Get it last, get it wrong, correct it and kill it!"

And the weather ball flashed rain.

CHAPTER TWENTY

IN MANY SMALL TOWNS EXISTS
a certain type of man who has polished the fine knack of ac-
quiring holdings to a fine sheen. He enjoys playing Monopoly
with real property, a game of widespread popularity, of course
—but he is locally the head-and-shoulders winner. He owns a
good percentage of the town's structures, and much of its land.

The secret of his success is, usually, a certain directness of
mind.

He knows the law of retail and wholesale and approves of it.
It is said of him that he knows the value of a dollar. In Bark,
Ark., his name is Purdy Dews and he owns the entire west
side of Main Street, the east side being a river, across which he
operates a ferry. In Wide, Arizona, his name is Jake Effton,
whose most recent venture into business was building a super-
market of which he said, "Actually, I hate to go into com-
petition with my father, but business is business."

In Flat City, his name was Elroy McIntosh and he liked to

preface remarks by stating sheepishly that he was just an old country boy.

"Well, I'm just an old country boy," Elroy said, standing on the shore of Devil's Lake outside Flat City, "Does seem, howsomever, a ninety-day option is worth lots more than the figger you said."

Yes, you're an old country boy, you old son of a bitch, John Riley thought angrily—like old Hitler used to be just an enlisted man himself.

John Riley had driven down to Flat City immediately after Cliff Tipton called him, the day after the dedication ceremony, to say he was ready to close a deal for the property across from Higgins.

Riley, who had not been at all idle during the summer, knew that McIntosh owned the north shore. The Higgins place was on the south shore. The west side of the lake down where the river came in was also McIntosh property and the east side—scraggly pines, overgrown palmettoes and sandspurs offered little possibility for a future turnover, so John Riley was concentrating on getting the entire north shore only. The huge, oval-shaped lake had only two rutted roads leading in—the one to Higgins' house and the one on the far north shore, from the old sawmill drag-out route.

Riley and McIntosh had driven in on the northern approach.

"Good lord!" shouted Riley, when McIntosh named his price. "Do you think this is mid-Miami? I just want an option —I wasn't talking about the purchase price."

"Do wish I could find who keeps stealing my no trespassing signs," said Mayor McIntosh, easing his new Lincoln carefully along. "The price of lumber these days, those signs don't grow on trees."

"Oh, all right," Riley said wearily. "You win."

"Funny you want an option way out here," said McIntosh innocently.

"Somebody's been stealing your signs, eh?" said Riley.

Both men were happy. Each knew the other was out to gaff him. It gave each a feeling of security.

Mayor McIntosh, shading his eyes, looked far across the lake and said, "Looks like the Higgins family out swimming. Want to drop by and say hello?"

"Uh, no," Riley said hastily. "Not today. I have to get back. Business."

"Uh huh," said Mayor McIntosh.

John stopped at the mayor's dry goods store long enough to sign the papers and whistled happily all the way back to Guava Springs. He answered several calls which had been left for him and called his wife that he had to go see a client. Then, he called Cliff Tipton and said, "All fixed, Cliff. I'll pick you up Saturday morning and we'll drive down."

"Is it the section with the big cypress trees?"

"Yes, Cliff."

"Good."

John Riley hung up, his face aglow. *Is it the section with the cypress trees?* Not *"How Much?"* Just, *"Is it the section with the cypress trees?"*

"Say not the struggle naught availeth," said John Riley, lying back against the sofa pillows.

"Say what, Johnny?"

"I do love a secretary in black toreador pants."

"I'm glad, Johnny."

"Shall we gather at the riverrrrr?" sang Mayor McIntosh in his store that night as he folded the option check and put it away. *"The beautiful, the beautiful riverrrrrrr? Yes, we shall gather at the rivvvvvver. Dum, dum de dum de dum de dummmmmmmm."*

Mayor McIntosh knew a secret.

He looked into the wall safe and the big fat check was there —the other check, the startlingly large check, the astonishingly large check.

It's funny, he reflected, how if a man just hangs on and isn't panicked every twenty years or so by what looks like a land bust how it all pays off in the end.

"*On the margin of the riverrrrr,*" he sang, shutting the safe, "*lay our every burden down. We will wait and worship everrrr, and provide a Golden Crown.*"

The day before Riley arrived to finagle the north shore property, Mayor McIntosh had sold, outright, the entire western shore of the lake down by where the river comes in. The purchasers had sounded like an awful strange outfit until he checked the credit rating. And found it excellent.

"Riley sure going to be one more surprised lad," said Country Boy McIntosh, lighting the thirty-cent cigar John Riley had given him, and counting the change in the petty-cash drawer. A man has to keep a close eye on detail.

CHAPTER TWENTY-ONE

Now august was ending and after only a very few months as a full-time writer, Paul Higgins found himself obsessed with his novel.

He had not set out on purpose to write a book. He had planned to wait a while longer. But over the years he had accumulated bits and pieces of chapters and scrawled notes and they had come to nag at him.

He had sold six short stories in the few months, for a respectable income. His output was increasing as his schedule settled down. And he found more time to spend on the book. The short stories had come to occupy almost the same position in his life as his public relations job had; that of furnishing livelihood—although with the all-important difference of being all his own and being done in a place he fully enjoyed. But he realized that he had to finish the first book before he could start a second.

Sometimes he thought the book he was writing might be a

good book and sometimes he thought it might be a poor book.

It was a story about an honest and hard-working business-man who succeeded by refusing to stoop to back stabbing.

"A cheap gimmick," Art had said. "You're simply doing it for the shock value."

Paul didn't think that was entirely it. It was more that he felt that a man who waited until he was forty-five years old to write a book must of necessity write an accurate one, based on his own observations. If a man was still very young it would be all right, he felt, to see drama in dope, wickedness in conser-vation of tradition, work his sex fantasies off in never-never lands of everyday orgies and tax-free sex, and all that sort of wishful thinking. Or, even if he were somewhat older, Paul could see how a writer might think there was nothing but a seamy side—particularly if he led a sheltered life like most of the "intellectual" writers Paul had known.

For the most part these latter associated mainly with their own kind, exchanging discoveries. Once in a while something bore out their most horrible suspicions, usually a faked-up love nest story in a tabloid, and they dearly loved to *portray life*. Some had even gone riding on a freight train! All had been per-secuted by life. Most scowled back courageously. None knew they were funny.

Paul had ridden on freight trains himself but he lost his cynicism after less than five years on a police beat and he never got it back. The disillusion was slow and it took quite a while to realize people were courageous and did the best they could, but once the cynicism left it could no more be regained than virtue. Sometimes he missed it.

But when it came to writing a book he felt that bouncing his theme off a sadist who owned a nympho who owned a heroin store was, basically, dirty pool. That bastards of all descriptions existed, Paul Higgins was quite well aware. He just didn't see the conflict—felt that juggling minority vice and ignoring ma-jority virtue would put him in the same league as a drama critic who utilized somebody else's creaton to knock off a cheap laugh in the early edition by a clever slam line. Bush league.

It was just a little too easy. Anyhow, Paul Higgins felt, that ever-loving seamy side was adequately taken care of, it seemed, in practically every new novel he read.

He preferred to write a book about a man, in the United States, who made out all right. Despite everything.

"It's certainly offbeat enough," Art said studiously. "Strictly from weirdsville. Maybe your sequel could be about a famous star who, in reality was a nice fellow."

"I wonder how Wedley's book is coming along?" Paul said to Art, who was seated on a stump down by the lake, drinking beer from a can and watching Paul and Tom Jedsoe unloading lumber from a pickup truck Paul had bought in midsummer.

"Fine, I imagine," Art said. "James A. Wedley has that greatest of all assets—no sense of the ridiculous, a completely self-centered man. He reminds me of an assistant city editor I used to know, name of Bertrand. His strong point was throwing press releases into the city room wastebasket. He threw away handouts for nine years in the newspaper business. Then he was hired by a public relations firm for lots more money."

"And started writing publicity releases himself?" Paul asked. "For other men to throw in wastebaskets?"

"Precisely," Art said. "And a good job he did. Until he lost two good clients in a row through stupidity. The PR firm fired him. He got his old job back. Said he couldn't get the old printer's ink out of his veins. Two weeks later he was on the desk throwing releases in the wastebasket. He picked one up and it looked familiar."

"He had written it himself!"

"Right. A detailed survey attempting to prove that beer is not fattening. He was torn. What to do? His assistant city editor self said toss it. His creative self protested, and admired the beautiful prose."

"Impasse."

"No," Art said. "Compromise. He worked it out to his satisfaction, edited it and sent it along. The editing was at a minimum. He simply knocked out a few words, thusly: Everywhere the survey said 'beer is not fattening' he edited out the word 'not.' Wedley would do that."

"What happened when the squawks came in?"

"Nothing. Bertrand would just holler into the telephone, 'Oh, yeah, don't give me that crap! I've got the facts! *You know, I used to be a public relations man myself!*' "

"A little learning is a dangerous thing."

It was shady late afternoon but the lake breeze had not yet blown the heat away and the two men, Tom and Paul, sweated under the timber which would be sunk for pilings. Paul was going to reinforce and extend the rickety pier.

There was beer in a bucket in the cool lake and they knocked off, sat down with Art to drink. Tom Jedsoe leaned back against a tree and looked through the woods at the Higgins home. The shutters had a new green paint job and the back porch had been painted barn red; with the sides of the house still weather-gray and the stockade roof trimmed in green around the edge, the big house had the look of a portly old sea captain, accustomed more to a faded uniform and slicker, suddenly finding himself in a strangely becoming admiralty dress and not even nervous about it.

"Boy," said Tom, "the old place looks good. I still think you ought to put in a truck garden."

"Why?" said Paul. "The local fad seems to be giving away vegetables. We've gotten enough from you alone to stem the India famine in a good-sized province."

"I'm just making up for chunking green oranges through the screens and windows here when I was a kid," Tom said, grinning. "A long-repressed guilt complex coming to the surface."

"You sound like a young lady I used to know in little theater," said Art.

"We used to use that staircase for a shot tower," said Tom.

"Drop hot solder down into a tub of water. It's a damn wonder we didn't burn the place down."

"Her name," said Art, "was Lou Higgins. Where is Lou?"

Rising, Tom said darkly, "I better be going. I've got to check my packing shed over near Oak Knoll."

He strode away down the path, his wide shoulders held rigidly, his walk angry. He swung up into the cab of one of his rigs, double-clutched down the sandy road.

"Did I say something wrong?" Art asked.

"Oh, no, not particularly," Paul said. "It's just that Lou rode into Fort Myers with that Jerry Space and Tom's all burned up about it. Where does my loyalty lie—am I supposed to be loyal to Lou, my flesh and blood, and say nothing, or am I supposed to be loyal to a fellow male and tip the stupid oaf that she's just trying to make him jealous?"

"Space?" said Art. "Where did he come from?"

"He's been down in the Keys," said Paul. "He is now spending a week in Fort Myers and interpreting the Tamiami trail. He dropped in earlier, while you were asleep, and invited her to ride over with him so he could explain the coastal highway system to her."

"And she went?"

"Don't worry. She knows a bad risk when she sees one."

"The pressure bit? She thinks Master Jedsoe might be a trifle slow in joining the family? What do you think of Tom?"

"He's a good boy," said Paul. "I like him."

"Don't think of it as losing a daughter. Think of it as gaining twenty-nine million tomatoes. That boy is going to end up owning this whole county."

"He says he doesn't want to be just a tomato farmer all his life."

"I wouldn't say a man with a fleet of GM trucks and a *carte blanche* credit rating was exactly a hardscrabble tenant farmer," Art said. "I'm going in and finish packing."

It was Friday. Art was leaving the next day. August was

nearly gone. Soon the summer would be gone from New York. Art was homesick now. He had written Otto and told him. The pavement would feel good. He had enjoyed the earth and the water, but too much of it, Art knew, would ruin him. A man could only take so much of no tension, then it started to tell on him.

Paul walked to the house with him. The sudden dark was coming. Upstairs, Paul sat on the bed and watched Art stuff clothing into his suitcases. Fine-grained leather, like the wallet on the bureau—the wallet with all the cards, so useless here; so important elsewhere. Down here, Paul thought, is a different galaxy.

Paul looked at the wallet and said, "Take my regards to your leader."

"What?"

"Nothing." Paul said.

"Oh. Oh, I dig you, Earthman. Get it? Dig? Earth?"

"That's enough, Art."

"This Martian lands, see? First human he sees is a British editorial writer. Martian slithers up to him and says, 'Take me to your leader.'"

"O.K., Art."

"Well, in England they call editorials 'leaders.'"

"Oh, shut your damn mouth."

For a fleeting instant Paul had a great yearning for many red and yellow lights and rivers of passing humans, with high heels clicking and strangers all around and the stimulation that is nowhere else to be found except in the city in the autumn at the twilight when the lights flicker on. But the moon hung low outside the window facing the lake and he knew he was only lonesome for where he hadn't been. The moon was orange, mottled orange behind the clouds of early Florida dark. I am going toward where I want to be, Paul thought; I have already checked the other out, and it wasn't that at all, wasn't there. He wondered where very old men wanted to go. Once, young, he had asked a white-bearded stranger on a green park bench, abruptly, "What are you thinking?" The old man said slowly, "I am thinking about what happened to the street cars." It had been an excellent, although basically uninformative, reply.

Paul looked at Art Rodes' sardonic profile and felt a tearing sense of loss that astonished him with its intensity. Now Art turned his back and, leaning over the suitcase a few seconds, suddenly turned to face Paul again. Standing there only in his baggy shorts, he had donned a bow tie and his communicative look and held a briefcase under one scrawny arm. He said, "Well, back to the old drawing board."

Paul grinned slightly.

"A needless prejudice has been built up against white slavery, Mr. Luciano," Art said solemnly. "The basic trouble is we aren't getting to the right audience—the profession still uses horsecar ad-placards in a subliminal-sell world. Let's toss this latest survey down and walk about it a bit. Now without getting into any fancy jargon like motivation research—I mean, hell, L.L., you're a businessman; there's no sense trying to impress you with esoteric terms. I mean while we've got some of the best minds in the business on this M.R. stuff over at Creation, I won't bore you with the details. Your secretary has a copy of the survey, I left it in the outer office. Actually, what is motivation research? Well, now you know and I know it's a new gimmick for an old truth. How did they sell lead at a good mark-up? They cast it in squares and painted it gold, right? Simple? O.K.—take the word white slavery, what word immediately comes to mind?"

Paul laughed, despite himself, despite the sadness and the tug of the quick near-tears. The crazy bastard, he thought, very sadly; for friends are seldom come by and distance always builds a wall. Art was on a different road forever now and Paul knew, all at once, that the two roads had forked in this very minute in an old house that was his home, oddly enough.

Art, quick, telepathic, felt it; changed the unspoken subject and Paul was grateful.

Art waved at the Unsell Chart still on the wall, at the Rodes-Higgins book of press clips. "I've been here less than a month and look!" Art said proudly. "In six months, after I get back at the national level, we'll have this place expelled as unfit for human habitation."

Art patted the scrapbook and said, "Keep the banner high. I'll keep in touch."

"I think Tipton must have changed his mind," Paul said. "He probably forgot all about it. I hope so."

"Be that as it may," Art said, "the situation may arise again. Don't slack up. What's running next week?"

"The piece you did on How to Identify a Coral Snake. When will you come back down, Art? Next summer? Maybe for Christmas?"

"Oh, I—"

"Paul," Betty called from downstairs. "Phone."

Getting called to the telephone now was a mild adventure instead of just one more abrasion of one more nerve.

"Hello?" Paul said expectantly, hoping it was his agent.

It was Cliff Tipton. He said he and his wife would be down in the morning, with John Riley. Paul said, weakly, fine. He hung up. He told Art, "He's coming."

"Oh-oh," Art said. "Well, get the pencils, kid. I can stay an extra day."

Rodes-Higgins stayed open quite late that night.

"I will tell him about the malaria epidemic," said Editor Willingham.

"Junior has an armadillo in his tree house," said Art. "Will not Mrs. Tipton be bemused to find it in her closet?"

"I will explain how to use the snakebite kits," said Paul.

"I will be proud of the progress against polluted water," said Willingham.

"What I wish we had is an alligator," said Art. "I don't know, though. It's not very subtle, is it?"

"It doesn't sing," Paul said. "It just lies there."

"Cough hollowly at regular intervals, everybody," Willingham said. "It's the dampness here."

Beneath the moon of Flat County that night the dark moss swirled and swayed in the small breezes that had survived from the outer rim of a hopeful little hurricane whirling far off the coast and trying to grow, whipping its way across a phosphorescent sea. Heat lightning arched and the sky was blotchy purple. The moon was dull and sullen.

Around the lake, in the fitful little wind, the leaves moved nervously; in the trees reflections and shadows writhed a little like questing inhuman things: It was a dandy night for monsters.

Jerry Space arrived home with Lou not very long after supper. Jerry had been, for him, courtly and gallant with Lou. Lou got out of his car, loudly trilling happy girlish laughter for the benefit of any big oaf around who just might be thinking he was the only pebble on the beach. But Tom wasn't in the house.

"He left," Betty said, as her daughter entered.

"Who?" said Lou brightly. "Jerry, how about some coffee?"

"Sure."

Upstairs, the members of the firm heard Jerry and Lou come in and, in sudden alarm, Art said: "He's not going to stay the night, is he?"

"No," said Paul. "At least he didn't mention it."

"One interview with Tipton by that character could undo everything," Art said. "Let's make sure he gets out of here tonight."

"By all means," said Willingham.

CHAPTER TWENTY-TWO

IN THE WONDROUS BALANCE OF nature, with its system of checks and balances, its wheels of punishment and reward, Gerald Space had led an exceedingly fortunate life—he was way ahead of the game. The night of the monsters, unfortunately for Jerry, not only evened the score but put him heavy loser.

It was the old story of the boy who cried wolf, but with a unique switch: In his case, everybody thought he was the wolf: a cruel irony. For once, he hadn't been.

All that day his every action with Lou had been entirely innocent and even his motives, if only out of an obvious hopelessness, were pure, or as pure as Jerry's motives could get.

Lacking the spur of the incentive system, and never entirely free of thoughts of the huge rube she went around with, Jerry —although he had eyed Lou with automatic hunger—had kept hands off and was for once, in a car with a good-looking woman, an absolute gentleman.

188

When Lou suggested coffee after he brought her home he didn't even ask for a drink instead. He was being a gentleman. When Lou suggested they walk down to the lake before he started the long drive back, he accepted with pleasure—but without his normal word-association of: Girls-woods-pass.

"I love to look at the water at night," Lou said, straining both ears for the sound of Tom's truck.

"Yeh," said Jerry. "Nice lake you got here. Big."

"If you want to rest before you start back," she said, "There are some camp chairs down the shore there, and back up in the clearing."

"O.K.," he said gallantly, and headed out down the bank, picking his way carefully, and trying not to think of snakes.

The heat lightning flashed and, back up in the woods, Jerry made out the clump of chairs. Walking carefully, the little knot tight in his stomach, he went into the woods. He groped through the trees, holding his hands out.

Something clasped his hands.

"*Heega!*" he screeched, jumping back; narrowly refraining from dropping dead. Something put a hand on his shoulder. The heat lightning flashed and he saw a monster in ragged clothing advancing upon him. He tried, unsuccessfully, to scream and, wheeling, ran full tilt into something large and alive—and in the lightning he saw a face which, under its strange headwear, would forever be in his nightmares.

The second monster had on a slouch cap.

It yanked at him.

They were fiends from hell, he could tell that, all right. For one horrible second he was sure he was surrounded; he knew there were at least two of them, evil smelling, tall, powerful, terrible—but in the next arc of lightning he saw the path to the lake was clear and, panting, slobbering, Jerry dashed from the woods. He was trying to scream but his vocal cords failed to operate.

Lou Higgins was standing on the shore by the pier admiring

the lightning on the water, when he raced up and grabbed her. She emitted a startled squall. He had grabbed her in the region of the chest, which, with Lou, was ample.

She turned and belted him solidly in the left eye.

"I've heard about you!" she shouted.

"No, no," he cried, pulling at her. "Come on, come on!"

"I will not and you leave me alone!" she squalled. Her blouse ripped open. Pausing only to deliver a right cross to his already swelling eye, she pulled loose and, screaming, ran toward home and safety, away from this obviously sex-crazed male.

He was right behind her.

And now, Tom Jedsoe, in clean clothing, scrubbed and shiny, had just parked his truck in the Higgins yard when, as he got out, he heard Lou shrieking.

Tom Jedsoe saw his true love galloping out of the woods, through the windy and dully-shining night, her blouse ripped open—and, ten paces behind, low to the ground and gaining fast, Tom saw Jerry Space.

"I knew what that bastard was the first time I laid eyes on him!" Tom Jedsoe gritted and, moving forward fast, stepped aside to let Lou pass and dealt Jerry Higgins a terrific belt in the right eye—the good one—which, what with Jerry's oncoming momentum, sounded like a baseball bat hitting a green watermelon. Jerry went back in a flat trajectory, ricocheted off a lime tree and dropped in a clump of sandspurs five feet off the path.

"No," Jerry whimpered. "Back there. Watch out!"

He got up.

Tom dropped him with a twelve-inch punch to the jaw. On his hands and knees, Jerry frantically tried to move on down the path. Tom helped him—planting a size 11-EE shoe in Jerry's rear end with a kick that would have sent a football eighty yards. It sent Jerry about six.

Then Tom picked up the city slicker and threw him into his automobile and said, "Get."

"Get inside," Jerry said, moving his swelling lip with some difficulty. "You don't understand. I saw—"

Jerry tried to get out once more.

"Boy," Tom Jedsoe said quietly. "I'll—"

"There are things in the woods!"

"Boy," Tom repeated. "You get, or I'll beat you slam to death."

"Don't hit him again, Tom," Lou cried. "He's had enough."

"Matter of fact," Tom said, "I think I'll beat *you* slam to death anyhow."

Jerry looked at the huge fist waving under his nose and, starting his car, shouted, "I'll save you from yourselves! Just keep her out of those woods until I get back!"

And he raced away as fast as his little car would carry him.

"What's happening out there?" Betty Higgins shouted into the eerie night.

"Yes, what?" said Willingham, coming out on the porch.

Paul Higgins, walking fast through his back door, looked at his daughter, wearing a ripped blouse, and at Tom Jedsoe massaging his knuckles. He heard the racing engine departing, took in the situation and said tightly, "He better not come back."

"You ain't just whistling Dixie," said Tom.

They heard the Space car hit the hard road and whine away toward Flat City.

"Maybe he *did* see something," said Lou.

"Lou Higgins," said Betty. "Get in this house!"

Jerry whizzed into Flat City doing 80; skidded to a stop at the first light he saw in an open store. It was Flat City Pharmacy and it was just closing.

Jerry raced in and telephoned the nearest Space paper collect—the one north of Fort Myers.

To the startled editor on the other end he shouted, "Goddammit, don't you argue with me. I know what I saw—and take this fast, word for word. I've got to get back out there."

"Well," said the young editor, who had not long ago replaced an old editor (who had been canned for putting Emerson's essays in the paper) and who did not want to be canned himself. "Well, O.K., Jerry. If you say so."

"Well I say so! Shut up and get this. I've got to get to the authorities and get up a posse!"

The proprietor listened the rise and fall of his crazy customer's voice: "Fetid smell . . . inhuman strength . . . toga-like garments . . . strange headgear . . . words incoherent . . . death breathed hotly on my neck . . . at least two of them seen with my own eyes . . . seemed to hear more crashing in underbrush . . . police to investigate . . . townspeople alarmed . . . looked like nothing so much as—as—as . . ."

Jerry Space, feeling a newspaperman's thrill with a big story, standing there with two black eyes and a fat lip a'wooing the deadline muse, suddenly realized what they looked like.

He told the editor what they looked like.

The editor sounded as though he were choking.

"That's what I said," Jerry said at the top of his voice. "That's the only comparison I can think of—and you goddamn sure better not change a word, unless you happen to hate your job. Oh yeah? Well, STOP the goddamn presses!"

He slammed the phone into the hook and shouted at the druggist, "Where's the police station?"

"Who's paying for that call?"

"It was collect, damnit. Where's the police station?"

"Well, you'll find the police chief across the street in the poolroom. However, young fella, I'd advise you get some black coffee afore you go around—"

But Jerry was running across the street.

Chief Williams had a straight-in shot to win the double or nothing big game—he would be even or sixteen games in the hole. He smiled smugly, chalked up and leaned over, sighting carefully. A real patsy. He drew back his cue.

"MONSTERS!" some bastard screeched in his ear just as

he shot. His cue stick ripped across the felt, missing the cueball entirely.

"Double triple damn!" yowled Chief Williams. "Oh double triple quadruple goddamn!"

Jerry Space said commandingly, "Quiet! Everybody listen!" The poolroom inhabitants heard a strange story, indeed.

Chief Williams' face, as he strove for some degree of control, having considered and discarded murder, looked like an over-inflated bladder. He was hammered-thumb purple. His entire countenance was the same shade as Jerry's darkening eyes.

"We'll need riot guns and flashlights," Jerry shouted, in conclusion. "We need a posse. Spread the word! Get the state police. Get the militia! Hurry up. Even now it may be too late. I'm getting back out there. Follow me, men!"

Jerry raced out of the poolroom and started his car, raced away.

Open-mouthed, the poolroom clientele watched him go.

Jerry Space, whipping down the highway, saw the red light of the police car behind him. Good, he thought, bending over the wheel. I have spurred them to action.

The flashing light gained.

It passed him.

The police car pulled him over.

"Get out of the way, Chief!" Jerry commanded. "Time is of the essence!"

The charges against him totaled: Disturbing the peace, going through a major intersection, using profane language, resisting arrest, assault with intent to do great bodily harm, attempted bribery, destruction of city property (a spitoon in the aisle en route to his cell) and going 91 miles an hour in a 20-mile zone.

"Will you please be quiet?" asked the jail's only other inmate, a Mr. Funnelthroat Freely. "Nobody can hear you anyhow, and I'm trying to do my bookkeeping."

Mr. Freely was to be released the following morning from a ten-day stretch prompted by riding a goat while under the influence of alcohol. He was estimating his assets. They totaled some $8.65, and the goat, which he liked to feel was his although he could remember with no appreciable degree of clarity where he had obtained it.

At any rate, he decided, it looked as if he would have to work a month or so. He did not relish the prospect, but he enjoyed his reputation as the only self-supporting village drunk in this era of creeping socialism and the welfare state. I guess I better work two months, he decided. That should get me through the winter.

"Oh well," said Mr. Freely, philosophically, trying to ignore the din in the adjoining cell. "Busy hands make happy hearts."

"The woods are full of monsters!" shrieked the man next door.

"Ever wake up riding a goat?" asked Mr. Freely, conversationally. But there was no talking to some people.

CHAPTER TWENTY-THREE

THE NEXT MORNING, ARTHUR Rodes was up early and feeling in excellent physical shape, a state of well-being which had astonished him each morning of his vacation down here. Mentally, too, he was keen. Ah, we have our work cut out for us today, he thought, and decided to go get the armadillo before breakfast.

"I will go get the armadillo before breakfast," he said, savoring the feel of the sentence spoken aloud, making a comparison: "I will go get the panda before tea. Before—ah, but I digress."

"What panda?" asked Junior, trotting outdoors with him.

"No panda," said Art. "A matter of rhetoric."

"What a character."

"What a character, sir."

"Yes sir. Why do you want the armadillo?"

"The seventy-five cents rental is not only rental, Junior. It is also payment for ask me no questions and I'll tell you no lies."

"Why do you want to go back to New York?"

The morning air was fresh, clean, damp. The night's rain still scented the air. Quail fluttered up. Art considered the question.

"Because New York is my home," he replied.

It was a half-mile walk to the tree house and Junior climbed up and brought the armadillo down in its cage. It was a cage which had been condemned for lizards, but was quite safe for an armadillo. It had a handle on it.

Art carried the armadillo. He strolled jauntily along. He rounded a large pile of brush which had been blown up against a fallen tree. Coming the other way were three men leading two large bears.

One bear was wearing a cap and the other bear was wearing a slouch hat. Both bears were wearing sweatshirts. On the sweatshirts was sewn: "See Wild-Wonder."

"Good morning," said Art. "I see you have some bears there."

"Have you seen a chimpanzee?" one of the men asked Art.

"No. No, I have not. I do have, however, an armadillo here."

Art felt he was carrying it all off rather nicely for a man who felt as if he had suddenly died and gone to hell.

"Hey," said Junior, "That's Mr. Hannegan! Hello, Mr. Hannegan." Mr. Hannegan looked at Junior dourly.

The bears moved in little circles.

Hippo Hannegan said to the bears, sourly, "Don't dance, no-goods."

"We been chasing these bear bastards most the night," said one man, the one wearing, of all peculiar apparel to be found on the shore of Devil's Lake on a summer morning, a plaid sport coat.

"They got away from us last night," said the third man, who was carrying a large press camera. "Is this your land? Maybe we ought to explain."

"We still don't find the chimpanzee," said Mr. Hannegan, worriedly looking up in the trees. "Here, Clarence! Hoo, Clarence! Ha, Clarence!"

"Clarence," muttered the man in the sport coat. "Fa cripes sake."

To the circling bears, Hippo Hannegan said, "By damn I said don't dance. You like for a boot in the butt?"

"Some trainer," muttered Sport Coat.

"I can explain all this," said the man with the camera. "I know it must look a little odd. Early in the morning and all."

Art held up his hand for silence. "Wait," he said.

The air was fresh, the leaves moved gracefully in the little breeze.

Arthur Rodes, deep in the woods of south central Florida, carrying an armadillo, contemplated the men he had met leading bears.

"Obviously," Art said, reading "Wild-wonder" on the bear's shirts, "you gentlemen are promoting something."

Sport Coat and Press Camera nodded mutely.

"Don't give me the mundane details yet," Art said. "I don't want to break the spiritual quality of this moment."

He contemplated the three men he had met leading two bears while looking for a chimpanzee.

"I want to savor the significance of this moment," Art said. "I want to shake your hands. Here, Junior, hold my armadillo."

The three men stared at him. They shook hands with him, as did the larger bear.

"In this moment, gentlemen, here in this wooded glade," said Art devoutly, "I believe the ancient art of publicity has come into its finest hour."

"Gee," said Sport Coat. "You really think so?"

"What a orator," said the man with the camera.

"Thank you," said Art, bowing slightly. "Now. One more thing."

"What?" said Coat, impressed by the spiritual overtones of it all.

"WHAT THE HELL IS GOING ON?" Art shouted.

"Hey, hey!" said Hippo Hannegan, warningly. "You wanna scare the bears? Hey—looky! Here comes Clarence!"

Far down the trail a reddish little chimp was waddling toward them, scratching its rear end.

At the house, Paul wandered around, somewhat nervously, waiting for Art. Art seemed to be taking an awfully long time just to get an armadillo out of a tree house. Paul sat down in the living room, listening vaguely to the voices of the women in the kitchen.

"I had wondered about those strange stories about this part of the state that I kept seeing in the Guava Springs Leader," Louise said to Betty. "You mean those two planted all of them? How utterly silly."

"Oh, it's not silly," Betty Higgins said, clanging down a skillet on the stove. "Not at all. It works, Louise. I happen to know that. I know it's hard to believe, but if you'd been around these public relations types as long as I have you would know that—silly as any given plan may look—it works."

"Oh, phooey," said Louise Antel.

Betty said, "Oh, it works, all right. Nevertheless, I resent anybody bringing a dirty animal into my house to scare people with and, furthermore, I will not put any guests in that leaky bedroom."

"You will too," Paul shouted. "You want this whole lake overrun with artists and people?"

Lou Higgins, helping her aunt with the biscuit dough—and the two of them looking much alike, stubborn-jawed, slim and sure of movement—said, "Well, I think the whole idea is just terrible, don't you, Aunt Louise?"

"Not so much terrible as silly."

Lou said, "Why, it would be just wonderful to have a famous writer right across the lake. I wish we had never moved down to this hick place. I hate it! And I'm going back to school at midterm, regardless of what I said before. And I'm going to tell Mr. Tipton on Father and Mr. Rodes, as soon as he shows up today. I'm going to tell him all about their stupid, stupid, stupid and dishonest thing. There!"

She slammed her fist down in the dough.

"No, Lou, you promised," her mother said. "You promised your father."

"You bet your sweet life you won't!" Paul roared, storming into the kitchen. "If you don't like the idea, go away for the day with your tomato baron or something!"

Astoundingly, his daughter broke into tears and rushed from the kitchen.

"Now what?" Paul said, amazed.

"You big flannelmouth," Betty snapped. "She and Tom had a fight last night. Maybe a permanent one. Lou, bless her gentle heart, got mad at Tom for hitting Jerry so hard until he found out, for sure, if maybe Jerry actually hadn't been just scared of something he thought he saw. You remember how just those little lizards drove him wild. Then Tom started saying the things all you men say when a girl goes for a perfectly innocent walk with another man."

"And comes back with a ripped blouse," Paul muttered.

"See?" Betty hissed. "See? You're all alike."

"Well dammit—pardon me, Louise, but your sister drives me insane—to hell! I've heard enough!" He opened the kitchen door to go outside. "You tell that girl that as long as she's my daughter I'll say who moves across the lake and not only to keep quiet but furthermore I have not built up this campaign for nothing and one word out of her and she won't know which side her bed is bruttered on!"

"The quotation you are striving for," said Louise calmly, "goes, 'She buttered her bread, now she can lie in it.'"

"Very funny," said Paul, with dignity, slamming the door behind him.

Louise watched him leave. Wonderingly, she said, "Did they really pay that man all that money in New York? Sometimes he doesn't act right bright."

"Oh, I know," said Betty wearily. "Everybody's so silly this morning."

Louise, putting on the kettle for coffee, said, "Betty, Cliff Tipton is a smart man—do you mean to tell me you actually think, believe, he will be swayed by a few attempts to misdirect his thinking about this beautiful place?"

"Sister. Dear sister," said Betty. "In the first place, Cliff Tipton is not a smart man. He's a writer. In the second place, why wouldn't he be swayed? The whole rest of the nation is swayed by people like Arthur Rodes. When the Rover Boys out there get through doing what they call 'sharing their thoughts on the matter' with him, you wouldn't be able to drag him to Devil's Lake. His thinking will be what they call 'constructively reoriented.' "

"Pshaw."

"Louise, I know it's difficult to comprehend. When Paul was newspapering we didn't believe in public relations. We thought public relations men were a bunch of racketeering ex-copy-deskers trying to justify their existence—sort of a cross between a literate con man and a witch doctor. Not so, Louise. It really works."

"Oh, Pshaw."

"No! One instance. Have you ever heard of Sparkilite?"

"It's the dependable one."

"You Can Put Your Trust in Sparkilite."

"I read about it in Reader's Digest."

"Well," said Betty, "with my own eyes I have seen that Art Rodes write a 3,500 word article on educational television and sell it to the Pacific Monthly—for the sole purpose of working in a plug for Sparkilite. He even managed to get in a survey result from a client company that makes camping tents."

"I don't take the Pacific," Louise said. "I do know the one

time I tried Sparkilite everything turned blue."

"I had the same trouble," said Betty. "But never doubt the influence of propaganda. You take that silly scrapbook they've compiled. By the time Cliff, or his wife, gets through—"

"What in the world is all that racket outside?"

Paul had slammed the kitchen door behind him and, unseeingly, was standing at the bottom of his porch steps, scratching absently at his chest. A strange car pulled into the yard and stopped by him. The occupants, four of them, stared curiously at him.

"This the place?" asked the woman, driving.

The man in the front seat said, "It don't look like it."

The woman in the back seat said, "Ask where is the ladies' room. My kidneys is floating, that drive from Fort Whatzit. Myer."

"You and the damn ladies' room—alla time," said the man in the back seat with her. "This is a wild goose chase."

"Yeh," said the man in the front seat. "What a foolishness. We could of been already in Miami."

"You got no sense advenshuh," his mate said. "So what's the hurry?"

"So where is the posse?" said the front seat man.

"So where is the militia?" asked the other man.

"Where at is the monsters?" the lady in the front seat asked.

"Where is the ladies' room?" her accomplice asked.

"Monsters?" Paul asked.

Suddenly, the front seat man screamed, "Hey, Sammy, hey, boy! Here they come now! Give a look, give a look!"

Paul looked toward his pointing finger. Bears were coming out of the woods, wearing clothing.

"Up widda windows!" screeched Sammy. "Up widda goddamn windows!"

Numbly, Paul stared at the parade coming like a blotched bit of surrealism across the fresh green morning.

First was Arthur Rodes, skinny, angular, sunburned, erect. Behind him was a huge bear with a hat and sweatshirt on.

Next came a man in a sport coat, with a long thin cigar in his mouth.

Next came Mr. Hippo Hannegan. He was leading a chimpanzee by the hand. Next came a great big bear with a cap and a sweatshirt on. This bear was waltzing absently.

Behind the happy bear was a man carrying a large camera.

At the tail end strolled Junior, carrying an armadillo.

Paul hadn't even had his first cup of coffee.

That was the only thought his brain allowed to leak through. I have been many places, his brain said very quietly, and seen many things. But I have to see this before I even have my first cup of coffee.

Then his next thought was: Betty will leave me and I don't blame her.

He started toward the parade. First he walked rapidly. Then he broke into a trot and he shouted, "Go back!"

"Pleasant morning, eh?" said Art. "You know, Paul, a funny thing happened to me on the way over to the armadillo this morning."

"Shut up," Paul said. "Get that zoo back in the woods! Betty is mad already about just one little armadillo! Junior, leave that bear's tail alone! Art, don't you have any sense? I don't know how you did this, but it's simply too much!"

"You mean it lacks subtlety?" Art said. "Doesn't have that certain quiet taste? You mean it doesn't gyroscope?"

Art looked toward the house and suddenly quit waving his hands in mock oration. "Hey," he said. "What's the crowd deal? Where they coming from?"

The first automobile had been joined by a black sedan, and a bright yellow station wagon was coming down the sand road.

"I don't know," Paul said desperately. "Just get those things out of here."

"They are not things, Paul," Art said. "And remember your

Southern hospitality. I want you to meet Mr. Mervyn and Mr. Must, two colleagues of ours in the publicity profession. And I believe you remember Mr. Hippo Hannegan."

A tourist dismounted from the yellow station wagon and, advancing warily, snapped a picture of the assembly and ran away.

Still another car was coming down the road. Then another.

The first four people to arrive had come tentatively down toward the lake.

"Them ain't monsters," said the lady who still hadn't been to the ladies' room. "Them's bears except for that monkey. And I don't know what that midget's got in the cage."

"It looks like a duckbilled papyrus," said her mate.

"I'm not a midget," said Junior, and turned to his father. "Shake hands with the big bear, Pop. The big bear shakes hands."

"You want to tell me about it now, Art?" Paul said. He was being self-contained. "I give up. Tell me."

"I'll tell you about the bears," said Art, "If you'll tell me where you got all these people."

A Cadillac from New Jersey was the latest arrival.

Mr. Mervyn and Mr. Must were elated when they read the newspaper story.

It was the talk of the coastal highway and still the curiosity seekers came.

It was by-lined:

By Gerald Space
All-Florida Correspondent

It told of monsters in the Flat County woods, of riot guns and posses, of strange beings sighted in the wilderness and it told it in under a splashy headline.

The headline in the Space paper said:

ABOMINABLE SNOWMEN
SEEN IN FLAT COUNTY?
POSSE COMBS WILDERNESS

"You didn't plant this?" said Mr. Mervyn, delighted.

"No," said Mr. Must, "It's like manna from home without writing."

Paul finished reading the gripping story and handed the paper back to a tourist.

"Abominable snowmen?" he said, his voice hasping.

"In south Florida?" Art Rodes croaked. Art recovered first. He said, "Well, they sure will have tough sledding down here."

"Why?" asked Junior, holding his armadillo.

Mr. Mervyn and Mr. Must were exultant. Here, they thought, would be a nationwide press play. They didn't understand it, but they were grateful, very grateful. For they were publicity men.

They had hired Mr. Hannegan, his chimp and his bears, to help obtain publicity pictures for their client, Wild-Wonder, Inc. The animals, wearing the sweatshirts plugging Wild-Wonder, had gotten away in the early dark and the press agents had looked for them until late, spent a fitful night in the Wild-Wonder truck, started the search again at dawn, come completely around the lake and found the bears in a clearing by some camp chairs.

Mr. Hannegan had been worried about his bears and threatened suit but he was happy now for he had bargained for time and a half for his bears. As for Mr. Mervyn and Mr. Must, they looked at the crowds flocking in, waving newspapers. It was a press agent's dream.

"What *is* Wild-Wonder?" Paul asked.

"The Wild-Wonder stuff wasn't supposed to be released until Monday," said Mr. Mervyn. "But I guess we better go ahead."

"What with the crowds and all," said Mr. Must.

"This is the kick-off campaign for Wild-Wonder," said Mr. Mervyn. "One of the biggest publicity drives in Florida history."

"Wild-Wonder?" Paul repeated. "What is it?"

"Paul," Art said gently. "Progress has come to Devil's Lake. Right across the lake, catty-cornered over there, will be quite an enterprise. Do you want to sit down?"

Mr. Mervyn and Mr. Must and Arthur Rodes told Paul, standing there in his nightmare, what Wild-Wonder was.

It was a corporation. It was to be operated by promoters with vast plans. Excursion boats based on Devil's Lake would travel the river.

"There will be glass-topped submarine rides," said Mr. Mervyn. Paul looked at him.

"A real natural-type layout," said Mr. Must happily. "Strictly from naturalville."

Art said, "And I believe you said it will have one of the largest monkey jungles in the world?"

"Monkeysville," said Mr. Must.

"Why here?" said Paul. "Why here?"

"So wild and primitive like," said Mr. Mervyn. "The corporation had been thinking of a place down in Collier County but—"

"Wait," Art broke in. "I better tell him. Paul, as bad as I hate to tell you this—"

Paul held up his hand. "They read about Flat County in the papers?"

"They read about it in the papers. . . ."

"Get those things out of here!" shouted Betty Higgins. "The bears, everything! Paul Higgins, I've had enough of this!"

The crowd was still coming. The abominable snowmen had joined paws and were doing a little dance. A tourist took a picture of the armadillo.

"Get in closer to the bears, Tammy!" a thin man with a camera shouted at his small and trusting daughter.

"What setting you using?" shouted a resident of Kansas City.

"F-16," the thin man called. "A little closer, Tammy."

"I might as well shoot that too," said Mr. Must, unslinging his camera. "It's got what you call human interest."

"Why will it be tough sledding?" Junior asked.

Hippo Hannegan took the large bear's hat off and put it in his paw. The bear walked toward the crowd, holding the hat out for donations. The crowd dispersed. The bear walked toward the Higgins porch.

"Make that bear go away, Louise," Betty said. "Louise, make it go away."

"It probably just wants to use the john, dearie," Louise said. "Everybody else does."

It was no place to try to talk, that was for sure, Paul decided. The circus atmosphere was mounting. He pulled Mervyn over into the trees. He slammed in question after question. It was neither joke nor pipedream; another Tourist Trap was coming in. The backing was sound and the plans well drawn.

"What Silver Springs has meant to the Ocala area," said Mervyn proudly, "Wild-Wonder will mean to this section of the Sunshine State."

Mervyn had all the facts at, as they say, his finger tips. He knew where there would be dredging and he knew where the offices would go up. He knew where the sight-seeing submarine base would be. He knew where the animals would roam. He said, "Even giraffes. In their natural habitats. Watching the boats come down the river. This section of Florida is going to amount to something. Foresight, that's what Wild-Wonder has got."

Paul stood there in the trees, watching the crazy panorama on his property. My Lord, he thought, half of Florida must have read that goofy story.

He couldn't get his thoughts straightened out.

Anger vied with sadness and sadness tried to smile.

Basically, he decided, his main trouble was a sense of the ridiculous. And still the monster-seekers drove in.

"Well," he said, "this should make your account very happy. It looks like a very good press, with the best yet to come."

"In*deedy!*" said Mr. Mervyn. "Nothing like publicity. Do you know where the hell that newspaper story came from?"

"Let's get some coffee," Paul said. "I need it."

"What will we do with the bears?"

"Oh, bring them, by all means."

That's one thing about public relations, Paul thought. That's the thing I never understood before—*that's* why it isn't dangerous, or frightening, or even immoral: There is no such thing as soft sell, hard sell, sweep sell, unsell, resell—any of them. He thought of all the tall buildings and the granite canyons. He thought of all the serious men, in the elevators. He thought of all the impressive surveys, the motivation research, the proofs that men bought convertibles in lieu of Paris mistresses. And all the other double-talk.

He thought, in short, of all the crap.

All those silly bastards, Paul Higgins thought, are carrying armadillos in their briefcases. And—sooner or later—every blessed one will meet two big bears coming around the other way. Take phrenology. Take blood-letting.

"What's funny?" grinned Mr. Mervyn, watching Paul.

Paul shook his head, clearing it, and looked at his lovely, despoiled homeland, where Progress was coming like fast hungry ants. The anger won.

And he said, "Nothing's funny, Publicity Man. Not one son of a bitching thing."

CHAPTER TWENTY-FOUR

Down the Tamiami Trail the Florida-seekers sped, scurrying frantically for relaxation, and down the Tamiami Trail this Saturday also sped John Riley, the Florida-seller, the real estate man.

"Cliff," he said, "You're making a wise move. You're moving into one of the few places left in the world where a man can have peace and solitude. That is very important in your work. It is very important in all our work. I read a book which said relaxation is just a state of mind. I thought that got right to the heart of the coconut, so to speak. What is your opinion on this?"

Tipton was snoring.

"He's been asleep an hour, John," said Trudy Tipton. "He's been on the wagon since the day before Progress and it makes him sleepy."

The Saturday afternoon was hot and on the coast smelled of burnt motor oil.

SEA SHELLS ONE MILE ON THE RIGHT
DON'T FORGET THE FOLKS BACK HOME
DON'T MISS ONLY ORIGINAL
SEMINOLE CORN DANCE
WATCH FLORIDA GROW
KEEP FLORIDA GREEN
SHELLED PECANS
10¢ ALL YOU CAN DRINK 10¢

John Riley turned toward Flat City and he said to Trudy, "Watch it change, now. You can actually feel the change start."

On the road to Flat City a sleek black car whizzed by him, honking like a Times Square news vendor; then another. Hm, thought John Riley.

"Speed Limit," said a sign in the middle of noplace, "20 MPH."

John Riley, wisely, slowed. A mile down the road Chief Williams had the tourist automobiles stacked back like cordwood. What the hell? said John Riley.

"This is peace?" said Trudy Tipton, as they neared the Higgins cut-off.

"Peace, peace, but there is no peace," said Cliff Tipton, awakening. "What time is it? Where are we?"

John was forced to brake to a stop at the road to the Higgins place. Cars were lined up.

"Get your souvenir chameleon!" a small boy named McIntosh shouted, poking a green lizard through the back seat window at Cliff.

"No," said Cliff.

Pop-eyed, John Riley watched two couples come out of the woods toward their car parked, with several others, off the highway. One of the men spotted a Pennsylvania tag on a parked car with people clambering out of it.

"Hey, Pennsy!" the man shouted, "Don't bother. It ain't no abdominal snowmen at all, it's just a couple shaggy bears taking up collections."

Tipton jerked upright in the back seat and, looking sleepily around, said: "Did I dream that? That is the most thought-provoking statement I ever heard." He looked at the crowds straggling in and out of the woods and inquired in a mild tone, "Where are we, John? Hell? Looks like the Sears exchange counter."

John Riley, his elbows on the steering wheel, his face in his hands, said only: "No. No no no. No no no no."

It was the biggest day Flat City had ever seen. Chief Williams got the entire civic machinery out of the red. Junior and the mayor's son, sold out of lizards, turned to hawking green citrus fruit. Reporters came from as far away as Miami. By mid-afternoon a farm editor from Tampa, who had decided a monster story fell in the livestock category, had arrived.

By late afternoon, most of Florida was shouting at the unwary: "Boy, those snowmen are going to have tough sledding down by Okeechobee, eh? Why? No snow. Yuk yuk!"

Dumbly, John Riley heard the story from Paul, when he and the Tiptons finally reached the house. And, as John Riley immediately and correctly theorized, Cliff Tipton didn't really want to build right next door to the biggest monkey jungle in the world.

But Riley, being a real estate man, heard Mr. Mervyn tell of his client corporation's plans and, once more, was elated.

"Say!" said John Riley to Mr. Mervyn and Mr. Must. "I got an option on that whole opposite shore over yonder next to Wild-Wonder. Some smart operator could get a tie-in and do a hell of a business with a, like, resort lodge."

"The cottages," said Mr. Must, "could be shaped like an African village."

"On stilts," said Mr. Mervyn.

"Saaaaaaay!" said Mr. Riley.

"You could call it 'The Safari Sands,'" said Mr. Tipton. "Where's the whiskey? Every time I go on the wagon something like this happens."

"In the kitchen," said Paul.

Cliff Tipton and Paul Higgins held up their glasses of straight rye.

"Down the drain, Paul," said Cliff. "You bitter?"

"Down the drain, Cliff," said Paul. "Yeh, I guess so."

"I was going to move here," Cliff said reflectively.

Paul told him about the hard unsell.

"Damn," said Cliff, feelingly. "This plays hell with you, doesn't it?"

"More or less. But not necessarily."

Paul broke out a case of rye for the press. What the hell, he figured. When in doubt, have a drink. The reporters kept the phone busy. They all had cute leads.

"Sit down with the bear, honey," the photographers said to the more shapely young ladies. "Could you get your dress a teensy bit higher, honey? That's it. Little more."

Mayor McIntosh came out. He said, "As mayor of Flat City, Mr. Higgins, I wish you to accept the sincere gratitude of our community. When it comes to publicity, sir, you are a miracle man."

"It was nothing."

Chief Williams staggered in near dusk. "Exhausted," he panted. "Been up to my ass in Yankees."

Art, always the media man, the communicator, had lettered two signs and nailed them on trees. The signs pointed to different sections of the woods and said "Snowmen" and "Snowwomen."

"Have a drink," said Paul. "You might as well."

"Sure," said Mr. Mervyn. "Here's cheers."

"Mud," said Mr. Willingham.

"Yee—ay!" said Mr. Tipton.

"You promised, Cliff," said Mrs. Tipton.

" 'A foolish consistency is the hobgoblin of little minds,' " said Cliff, nailing back his drink. "My God, this living room looks like Disneyland."

Reporters were still fighting over the telephone. Total strangers wandered in and out. But the crowd was thinning. The chief accepted a drink.

"To increased horsepower," he toasted. "Say, any of you know a lunatic named Space?"

"Where is he?" Paul said.

"In jail."

"Damn!" said Paul. He felt guilty. He explained what had happened and said to Chief Williams, "I'll pay any fine, put up any bail. But get him the hell out of there."

"Under the conditions," said Chief Williams, "there is no fine. I'll go get him myself. I owe that boy an apology—this day has been the high point of my entire career."

"Drive carefully," said Art, as the police chief left. "And bring a couple of cases of beer as commission for the publicity bureau."

The chief left for Flat City. By dark the last strange car had vanished, except one driven by a Nathan Norris, a leather goods man out of Ocala, who insisted on waiting to see the bears leave. He was under the impression one of them drove the truck. He was terribly disappointed to see Mr. Mervyn get behind the wheel but was mollified when Mr. Must agreed to get in the back with the animals and Mr. Hannegan and let one of the bears sit in the front seat.

"Good-bye, good-bye!" shouted Mr. Norris, waving at the departing truck. "You've made my day for me! I want you to know that."

"Godspeed!" called Arthur Rodes after his colleagues in the profession. "Congratulations on a job well done!"

Art, Paul, Louise Antel, the Tiptons and John Riley were

seated in the littered living room when Chief Williams returned with a battered and despairing Gerald Space. Chief Williams had a case of ale on each shoulder.

"What will I do?" Jerry whimpered. "I'm ruined. The laughing stock of Florida."

Paul and Art and Willingham looked at one another.

"The least we can do," said Art, "is to shut down Rodes-Higgins with a bang."

"What is our audience?" said Paul. "What is the desired image?"

"You write the story," Willingham said to Art. "You're the best liar. Paul can edit it down to believable proportions. I'll call it in to the Space papers—they'll believe me."

It was an excellent story. It told how Jerry Space, alone and unarmed, had pursued what to anybody would have appeared to be inhuman monsters. With only a flaming torch he had chased these bears from a helpless girl, and suffered severe contusions and abrasions in the dark of the forest. The Flat City Publicity Bureau was quoted as saying Gerald Space deserved a special award.

The local editor was quoted as saying, "As long as there is a Flat County it will remember the name of Jerry Space!" Jerry's long absence was explained by stating he had been mired in quicksand.

Inasmuch as the story was the only one which had the full details of start of construction of Wild-Wonder, which in itself was a legitimate news story, the article which would appear about Jerry promised to make the other stories look a trifle silly.

Willingham dictated the last sentence to the editor at the Guava Springs office, headquarters of the William Allen White of the Sunshine State. "That's right," the old editor said, "After a night and day of exposure to the insects and marshes of Flat County, after chasing, bare-handed, these animals far back into the marshland, Jerry Space was able to mumble modestly, 'Anybody would have done the same thing.' Got it? O.K. Send

the check to me care of my office and include $38 expenses and
fifty-six miles mileage."

"You'll be a hero," Art said to Jerry. "Don't forget now. You
paused only to call in your story, then went bravely out into the
night. Hm. I don't know about those shiners. I suppose you
could say one of the bears jumped you."

"A fitting swan song to a beautiful relationship," Willingham
said to Paul. "Our very own hero."

The hero suddenly got up and ran full tilt into the wall.

"Why did he do that?" asked Chief Williams.

"There's no front door," explained Cliff.

Jerry cowered in the corner, looking fearfully at Tom Jedsoe
standing in the kitchen door.

"Whoa boy," said Tom. "Ease off. No sweat. I'm sorry I
belted you before."

Tom was standing there with one arm around Lou and the
other arm around Betty.

Mrs. Higgins said, smiling, "These two want to announce
that they are going to be married."

It was a fine engagement party.

Very late that night Paul and Betty Higgins walked down to
their lake. Jerry and Willingham had gone and so had everybody else, except the Tiptons. Everybody in the house was
asleep, except Tipton, who was doing his three hours on Paul's
typewriter.

Paul and Betty sat down in canvas chairs in a clearing. Behind them the huge house rared above the grove of scrub oaks
with their hanging moss. The house looked out over the black
lake and the river mouth.

Serenely, Flat County lay, quietly and anciently calm. The
hump-backed cattle mused in the dark, the mango trees let
fruit go with little plumps of sound. Guavas fell. Palmettoes
fidgeted and over Flat County the moon was thin and pale and
sharp-edged.

Soon now, Paul thought, the bulldozers would come.

"Well," he said to his wife, "here we are."

"Yep."

"They got us, kid."

"How sad are you going to be about it all?"

Paul looked at his lake.

"Over that way," he said, "we will have Wild-Wonder, Inc., with all its natural wonders including, I imagine, a public address system. And across there, if John Riley is half the promoter I know he is, we will have a lodge which wouldn't look out of place in Mau Mau country. Except I rather imagine it will have outboards emitting from it, with fat ladies on water skis. That leaves only the west shore empty, down where the turpentine pines are."

"That land may turn out to be quite valuable," Betty said, "if the road gets built through to the Clewiston cut-off."

"What? How do you know?"

"Tom told me. He has an option on the tract. If the road project goes through he's going to put up his own tomato processing plant there. He doesn't want our daughter to be married to just a produce man."

"A tomato processing plant?" Paul said.

"A catsup plant, darling. Our son-in-law is a comer."

"The south is becoming industrialized rapidly," Paul said.

Under the moon he sat. Monkeys and motels and catsup, Paul Higgins thought. How sad am I? Very sad.

"Where can a man go any more?" he asked his wife and the night.

"Well," she said, taking his hand. "We could go swimming."

He decided he would be enraged at her insensitivity. He thought perhaps he would rail that she never had understood him. He might work in, he pondered, the bit about the suffering artist caught in a world he never manufactured—and perhaps close on a bellowed note of hopelessness: The what's-the-use? business.

He looked at her, under the moon, the woman who had followed him or led him through many odd situations, and she was smiling a little one-sided sad smile. So he kissed her, comforting her, and said, "By God, that's the thing to do. Go swimming."

So they did, and floated on their backs and looked at the sky over the lake which was still, for a little while, theirs, and peaceful.

At the airport the next day, Sunday, Art shook hands with Paul and said, "Well, it would have worked, the unsell."

"Except the bears came around the other way."

"That's the wonderful thing about publicity work," said Art. "You always come up against an angle coming around the corner, and so you never run out of a job."

"It is part of the wondrous balance of nature."

"You bastard." Art grinned, and walked toward his plane. Then he turned, and asked Paul, "What are you going to do now?"

"Me? I'm a writer. I'm going back home and write."

"Blessings."

And Paul watched the plane roar up and then away to Groson's where the martinis and bracelets tinkle; imported gin and costume jewelry, tribal fetishes of the quick people.

"Ready to go, kid?" he asked Betty.

"Any time," she said. They drove back home.

CHAPTER TWENTY-FIVE

Three days past his forty-sixth birthday anniversary, Paul Higgins stood at the rail of a tall ship, looking back at the United States of America. He watched New York leaving.

Down the rail a divorcée going to Paris stood at the rail and looked at the big man with the gray-black hair, wearing no hat, deeply tanned. He was lighting one mentholated cigarette from the end of the old one and squinting through the smoke. He felt her looking and gave her one skilled, approving, up and down look. This, the divorcée thought, will do fine for a start. Then she frowned as an obvious wife-type joined the big man at the rail.

"My, what an interesting view," said Betty and he looked at her sharply. But she seemed to be watching New York.

It had been six months now since the snowmen came. It had been five and a half months since the first bulldozer came to Devil's Lake. On a clear day he had been able to see it from his upstairs window. Wild-Wonder was coming along fast.

217

Foundations were being put in for the Safari Sands. Tom Jedsoe was laying out plans for his factory. Paul had finished his book. Now it was winter; another year.

His book had been accepted, rather reluctantly.

It would be published in the fall. He had the first draft of his second book in outline. He had just sold a short story. It was about a man who saved clichés. Now he and Betty were going to Europe, because they had never been there.

It was afternoon and the wind smelled like green salt. Behind him walked a woman leading a dog in a purple sweater. Paul felt good, and free, and independent. He had set out to be independent, writing, and it looked as if he were going to make it. He was happy about that.

Lou and Tom were happy, and he was happy about that, also. Junior was being taken care of by his aunt. Junior now said yes-ma'am habitually.

"Feeling good?" asked Betty.

"Sure am."

He looked down again at the book Art had given him for a going-away present. He read the jacket again.

". . . this searing insight into the empires ruled by power-mad mind merchants . . ." he read. "With startling, frightening clarity is drawn the portrait of a ruthless tycoon, a relentless moulder-of-opinion for hire to the highest bidder. In this, his first novel, James Aaron Wedley has lain bare the passions and vices of the men and women who scamper through the Headache Honeycomb of Madison Avenue, exposing . . ."

Paul grinned.

Then he sobered. What will I do when we get back? he wondered.

I have a house in New York, he thought. And it looks as if I always will, if I don't come down on the price. I have a house in Florida. I can go either place.

He thought of Cliff Tipton and wondered how he was doing. Cliff and Trudy had moved to an island off Cuba, and Cliff, dead-panned, had released the news to the press that he was researching an exposé of tuna fishermen. He had written Paul that he was living in a lighthouse. He said he had advertised for a light housekeeper, but unsuccessfully.

Paul lit another cigarette. What will I do? he asked himself. Go work in the tall buildings again, if my book flops? Not necessarily. Move away from my lake, because it will be crowded?

Maybe, he thought. And maybe not. He looked across the water at the United States.

Back there, he thought, he could do anything he wanted to do and was able to do. Back there a man can do anything he has the guts and skill for. Nowhere, he thought, during any time in history, have there been so few confinements and shackles. A very brave free place.

"Betty," he said. "What the hell am I going to do in that place out there when I get back to it?"

"I don't know," she said, happily. "What do you want to do, Grandpap?"

Well, Paul Higgins thought, flicking his cigarette butt at the tall buildings—that's one thing about the whole magnificently goofy setup. A man can do what he damn well pleases. Good.